JFP

This ite
charges

BROKEN WORDS

B R O K E N   W O R D S
Helen Hodgman

Published by VIRAGO PRESS Limited 1989
20-23 Mandela Street, Camden Town, London NW1 0HQ

British Library Cataloguing in Publication Data

Hodgman, Helen, *1945–*
Broken words.
I. Title
823 [F]

ISBN 1-85381–010–X

Printed in Great Britain by Bookcraft (Bath Ltd)

This book is for BARBARA. With thanks to JANE CAMERON, ROGER HODGMAN and NATHAN JONES. And with special thanks and love to MEREDITH HODGMAN for telling me about the ducks.

The pond on the Common froze in the night. Thirteen ducks were caught by their feet. The big dog came along and bit each bird off at the knee. Later, the sight of a stubble of duck stumps poking through the ice like a five o'clock shadow was to fracture Hazel's morning.

Harold turned up again on the morning of the duck slaughter. He stood on the doorstep looking depressed. His orange robe was ragged. His shaved head was taking on a purplish bloom because of the cold. Moss wouldn't let him in. He'd lost his key long ago.

Moss didn't tell Hazel about Harold being back but Hazel told Moss about the ducks.

Sun and moon hung together in a pale sky as Walter stalked the Common with a big stick.

'Angst!' cried Walter, 'Angst, Angst, Angst!'

Walter had come by Angst at his wife's insistence.

She'd become nervous at having large sums of money in the house, as was often the case in Walter's business, so she'd loaded the two youngest into the Renault and driven to Poole, Dorset, where an old WAC chum of her mother's kept a kennel, and got the dog for a song. The old WAC chum was only too happy to see it go.

Walter would have liked to say they'd been sold a pup but didn't. This was precisely the type of joke that brought out the worst in his wife.

It was she who had named the missing German shepherd Angst. Her own name is Daphne.

It would soon be dark.

Hazel lay in bed listening to the tinny tick of Moss's alarm clock. Downstairs someone rattled the front door and shouted something through the letter-box that she didn't quite catch.

'Don't answer the phone,' bossed Moss in her sleep.

Harold wept among the black plastic rubbish bags in the gutter. His knuckles ground his tears to shimmering bits bright enough for him to see all his faults by.

He wished he could grab this night and slit its throat. He began walking, heading in the general direction of Clapham South.

Three streets away the dog chewed the toes of a drunk asleep on the steps of the public library. There was nobody about.

Moss gave Hazel a nautilus shell, explaining that it was a tropical mollusc and had within it many self-contained chambers, each of which marked a period of growth. Moss put it on a plastic stand and placed it on the mantelpiece. She kissed Hazel, softly intruding her tongue into the two pink corners of her lips. Hazel began to cry. Moss took no notice. Hazel tended to cry on her birthday because, no matter what anyone gave her, it was never, never enough.

Elvis shoved Hazel in the stomach.

'You're no good,' he howled. 'You don't play.' He gave her his ball. 'Throw it!'

She threw it. He took off across the grass in pursuit but was beaten to it by the big dog. Elvis tripped and lay roaring up at the sky.

'Bad dog,' he scolded. 'I want my Mummy.' It began to rain.

Elvis cried during his bath and his baked beans on toast. Hazel thought this must be because he'd lost his ball, but it turned out that while he'd been playing outside that afternoon a bald man in a torn dress had jumped out from behind the trash and begged Elvis to call him Daddy. Hazel said they ought to call the police.

'You don't know what you're saying,' scoffed Moss.

She had a wide smear of tomato sauce across the bib of her dungarees. The phone started to ring.

2

'Why don't we answer the phone any more?' asked Hazel.
'Because,' said Moss.

Hazel was having her car-wreck dream again.

A man in a slightly shiny red jacket proposed lifting her up.

'Take a deep breath,' barked a woman in curlers.

Hazel felt big cold tears rise in her eyes and woke. Moonlight fingered the faces of a collection of smooth white dolls huddled on the window-ledge. They'd each come back to her marked 'Return to sender'. She'd plucked out their hair, picked out their eyes and painted each one white. She'd used a flat plastic paint.

Apart from that she'd done nothing, because there was nothing to be done.

Elvis buried himself in the sandpit while Hazel stood admiring her shadow on the concrete. It made her seem tall and substantial, though not so substantial as the man who came up behind her and asked if she'd seen his dog.

'We've met before,' said Hazel.

'I think not,' said Walter, raising his shapeless, tweedy hat.

Harold was getting cramps in a phone box in Tottenham Court Road.

'Nine hundred and ninety-nine,' he chanted. He had to get through to explain his position. It was a sad child that didn't know its own father.

A girl in a navy blue blazer tapped on the glass. She gestured at him with a carnation. Harold hung up.

It was dark when Hazel brought Elvis home. Moss was worried.

'Where've you been?' she demanded, tugging at Elvis's wellingtons. A trickle of sand poured onto the rug. 'What've you been doing?'

'Seeing a man about a dog,' Hazel told her.

3

One cat sat on the ironing board. The other cat was out. Hazel sat reading in front of the fire. Moss sat in the opposite armchair, catching up on some mending.

A tile slid from the roof, smashing on the concrete path at the side of the house. They didn't usually do that. Usually they slid into the guttering and Moss climbed up and put them back in place. Perhaps part of the gutter had come away.

Moss sighed. She doubted she could fix it by herself, and repairs were so expensive. She secured the little Noddy button that held up Elvis's trousers and draped them on the fire-guard so they'd be nice and warm for him in the morning, while Harold quietly forced the bedroom window and climbed inside.

He felt along the wall and found the light switch.

She'd got rid of their bed and replaced it with two single ones, placed side by side with identical burgundy duvets.

'How chaste,' he snarled, looking around for something to smash.

Although he had nearly fallen off the roof, he was feeling better, more able to cope. He put it down to the girl with the carnation who'd handed him the bit of paper that changed his life. Also, his hair was growing back.

Upon discovering the mess in the bedroom Moss thought it only sensible to tell Hazel that Harold was back.

'What gets up my nose,' she said (and not for the first time either), pummelling her pillows and trying to get comfortable, 'is his sodding off to India like that in search of enlightenment and leaving me holding the baby. Not to mention all those bloody bills. What's this? I don't have my glasses.'

Hazel took the crumpled leaflet Moss had found under her pillow and read: 'What is Scientology? All we know of science and religion is based on . . .'

'Oh, spare me,' groaned Moss. 'Honestly. I don't even want to think about it.'

4

Nor did Hazel. Instead she thought of Walter.

'We should get a dog. A big one.'

'The way we live wouldn't be fair to a dog. But I will have the locks changed. How about that?'

Hazel didn't think there was much point and said so, but Moss was already asleep.

Walter had so many children he didn't know what to do. He didn't need another.

In spite of her denial he knew Hazel had been lying in wait for him outside the tube just now — and waiting some time, by the look of her hair, which was so slick with rain it could have been painted on.

God only knew why he'd made the mistake of asking her in for a drink, he thought gloomily as he sat in his basement kitchen pouring her another while she went to the lavatory.

Hazel flushed the toilet, slipped off her clogs and crept about the house. She liked it. It looked cosy. 'Lived in' was the term, she thought. Lots of books. Pictures. Caution kept her from the top floor, where an unsteady thump of drums warned that at least one of Walter's sons was at home.

By their third drink Walter was letting himself remember how, that day on the Common, she'd struck him as something he might want.

Hazel smiled at him sideways and sipped her Scotch. Walter reminded himself that he had no intention of ever dialling the number she'd given him. Life was too short. He had to get that dog back before it did any real damage. It had already taken up too much of his time. He had a business to run.

Elvis squatted under the clothes-line doing his best to set fire to a heap of leaves with matches he'd taken from the shelf above the stove. He went through all but two without success. Prudently, he put these in his pocket for later and gave it up as a bad job.

5

He drifted away in search of amusement.

Five minutes later his mother saw him from an upstairs window, trying to force himself through the sticky privet that guarded the front of the house next door.

Seeing him so aimless made Moss want to run down and shake him. She felt the familiar pinch of guilt, a sense of strain in her dealings with him that she did her best to beat down. Sometimes, fleetingly, Moss would have liked to talk over her darker thoughts with Hazel, but Hazel considered herself to have cornered the market on those and didn't wish to share it. Moss smiled. In general she felt herself to be strong, unlike Hazel who was a disturbed person. Just how disturbed it was difficult to say. Moss had stopped worrying about it. Everyone was fucked up. It was just a matter of degree.

Elvis had disappeared.

Moss hoped Hazel would be home in time for tea. There was cake.

Hazel had gone to the National Portrait Gallery to sober up by looking at that picture of the Brontë sisters and then, on the tube going home, she'd thought everything over, deciding not to mention Walter to Moss who had already set a precedent for deceit by being so cagey about Harold.

Moss and Hazel had money worries.

Hazel was all in favour of renting out the downstairs front room. Moss thought that keeping her freelance graphic-design work quiet was enough of a con. DHSS grasses (Mr and Mrs Fisher next door) would be laying anonymous complaints against them if they tempted fate further.

Besides Hazel was overlooking certain things.

Moss reminded her that it wasn't all that long ago that the three of them would have starved if it hadn't been for daily visits to the Bin of Life in Covent Garden. Now, thanks to the above-mentioned work, they could go shopping like normal people.

6

What's more, the council had waived the rates and the DHSS had taken over the mortgage due to her deserted status.

Moss was confident that in the fullness of time things could only get better. Hazel snorted. She wasn't big on the fullness of time.

Harold paced his dingy digs, considering his options. Things weren't working out. If he had his own premises he could start his own religion, but Moss was lodged like a blackhead in the only place he'd ever come within spitting distance of calling his own.

Harold crossed to the window and began counting the bricks in the wall opposite. His new-found friends were making him nervous. He'd caught rumours of how they dealt with those who fell by the wayside. He found comfort in the fact that he'd given them her address as his own which, after all, was nothing short of gospel.

Some woman had just crossed the Alps on an elephant.

Hazel glared at Moss over the top of the *Guardian*, the cramped look on her face making her appear older than her years.

Hazel wanted an elephant and her photo in the paper.

She wanted a swimming pool too, in which the water was always 85 degrees.

She wanted clear blue skies and distant glimpses of mountains.

She wanted —

Hazel struggled to be practical; considered taking something with the Open University, a thought that promptly tipped her into tears.

'Now what is it?' asked Moss.

'I don't know.' And she didn't. Life had no plot, that was all.

'Here's a thing,' cried Moss, tapping the back page with an eggy teaspoon. 'Just listen to this. It says here that women who have a lot of sexual partners when they're young are more likely to get cancer. Sperm's a carcinogen. They've proved it.'

'I thought they'd proved that a long time ago,' said Hazel.

'They said there was a possible connection, but nothing was certain.'

'Well, it never is,' said Hazel.

'And now they've studied some nuns and they've proved it.'

'How?'

'Nuns don't get cancer.'

'I should've been a nun,' said Hazel.

'They're all dykes, you know.'

'All the more reason,' said Hazel.

'Do you love me, do you? Do you love me? Do you need me? Will you never leave me? Will you make me so happy the rest of my life? Will you take me away and will you make me your wife?'

At first it had been love.

Curiosity, that more adult refinement, came later.

Ground into the dry earth of somebody's father's paddock, sweat-glued onto the leatherette back seat of somebody's father's car. School nights, her body hot and numb, her mind free to wander, to set up its own wild wailing.

Jeez Haze.

In Elvis's room floral curtains, thin and frayed, fell to within an inch of the sill. Moss was always meaning to replace them, but she never got round to it until Elvis forced her hand by setting them ablaze.

Alerted by the smell, Moss took the stairs two at a time to find him squeezed behind his door, legs crossed, thumb in mouth, cheeks slick with excited tears. Moss told him that if he ever played with fire again she'd kill him.

Elvis nodded.

'An eye for an eye, a tooth for a tooth!' he droned sleepily.

'Honestly,' said Moss to Hazel later, 'where d'you think he gets that stuff from?'

He got it from the Bogeyman who had the words MADE IN ENGLAND tattooed on his penis in a wrinkly sort of morse code.

Sometimes the Bogeyman let him play with it and then it stretched out so's you could read the writing. Elvis' teddy bear had the same thing printed on its label.

The Bogeyman lived in the boarded-up house at the end of the street. It was Elvis's most secret wish that this person was his Dad, and not the man in the dirty frock who'd given him such a fright.

But Hazel knew none of this and so couldn't answer, and anyway Moss didn't believe in Bogeymen or Daddies.

Once upon a time, in a summertime which wasn't much of a summertime, the times being what and when they were, five-year-old Harold had gone to the pictures one Saturday afternoon all by himself. After that chicken had come on and sang cock-a-doodle-doo, the screen had filled with ugly puppets thrown in a heap on somebody's allotment (was it?). Bulldozers were pushing the ugly puppets into holes, where they flopped and bounced all over each other while soldiers just like his Dad stood watching with their hankies over their mouths. Everyone in the cinema had wriggled and lit cigarettes, except one man in Harold's row who'd laughed and lots of people had turned round and hissed at him.

Harold had asked his Dad about it next day when they were down the allotment and his Dad had begun to cry, so Harold had cried too and then his Mum had come to tell them their Sunday dinners were getting cold.

'What have you been telling him, Sid? What've you been saying?' she wanted to know, and all in that high, tight voice that meant trouble.

His mother had hit his father, who'd turned white except for the shape of her hand in pink upon his cheek. Then she'd reached out that same hand and ruffled the top of Harold's funny little post-war haircut and told him to run along. He hadn't wanted to leave his father weeping on an up-turned bucket, but he had.

'You shouldn't carry on like this,' he heard her say. 'I know the war sent you barmy, but you should make an effort for his sake. Never mind me.' And then she'd started crying too.

Hazel sat in the bath shaving her legs and brooding over the loose ends of her life. The child, for instance. The little Lucienne, held incommunicado in Canada by her father, le Professeur de Judo, and mourned by the ghostly grieving dolls upstairs.

The constant sweep of traffic along the road round the Common was stilled by 3 a.m.

A chocolate-coloured Rover glided to a stop outside No. 20. A young man wearing a three-piece suit of crushed Italian cotton eased himself from the back seat. He stepped lightly in his plimsolls up the garden path and popped something through the letter box. The chocolate-coloured Rover slid away from the kerb. The young man skipped along the pavement, whistling, before hurling himself back in beside the uniformed driver. The car turned left at the launderette, swerved to avoid the big dog standing in the middle of the street and surged away in the direction of the market.

Harold stuck his fingers in his ears and stared at his own front door from his vantage point behind the low front wall of the house opposite. He looked with regret at the smart blue paint and the four glass panels — the two bottom ones covered in bright vinyl with a camel and palm-tree motif, the two at the top frosted.

The door moved towards him, hung quietly in mid-air and then crumbled. A dull boom shook the street. Harold bolted before the dust settled.

Elvis gouged his Weet-Bix.

'Ground Zero,' he muttered at Hazel, who didn't hear him, her ears being strained to catch whatever it was Moss was telling the police constable in the front room.

She looked past Elvis, past the spindly avocado plant Moss was trying to grow on the window-ledge from a stone stuck in a jam-jar, through the big window and out into the small square garden.

Moss worked hard in this garden. It gave her a lot of pleasure. She had fitted mirrors behind the honeysuckle trellis on the back wall and was very pleased with the effect.

In summer the garden brimmed with flowers but now the only

splash of colour was the red canvas deckchair Hazel had forgotten to put away come autumn, which was now too warped to worry about.

'Boom!' yelled Elvis.

'Shut up,' advised Hazel.

The police constable left and Moss came in.

'Well?'

'Nothing.'

'It wasn't me,' said Elvis. Moss laughed and held out her arms to him.

'How about a cuddle?' she said.

In Vancouver, British Columbia, le Professeur de Judo howls in his narrow bed behind the bead curtain. He has his own version of things, wrapped in dreams so mean they chip his teeth. Scrambling blankets about his ears he shivers his way through realms of ice. It is cold up there. Freezing air burns his nose, catches at the back of his throat, causes his eyes to water, causes distant city lights to go runny as though the very world was bleeding to death beneath his dangling feet. The chair-lift sways, and oh how she clings to him. There are tears in her eyes too, but he will not be touched by them, knowing cold is their only cause. Her nose runs as she snuggles against him, smiling with wind-chapped lips up into his face. The gun is in his hand. How? How did it get there? Those lips move, twitched by shock into the shape they once had made to receive his kiss. And so, thinking of happier times, he shoots her and wakes to find the morning overcast. Like the morning she'd left, telling him she was just stepping out for some cigarettes — a detail for which he will never quite forgive her.

Le Professeur de Judo no longer believed in the possibility of the daily practice of ethical love. Hazel never had.

The first thing Harold saw on waking in the ditch was the blunt calligraphy of gravestones hammered on the horizon. He stretched and stood to pee, his eyes level with the top of the hedge.

On the far side of the neighbouring field a flock of starlings followed a tractor, wheeling first one way and then another, opening and closing ranks, flashing an uncrackable code across the day's clean face. Harold, for one, couldn't work it out.

He considered it a minute, licking furry teeth. Then he stuffed himself through the hedge and went to seek directions from the tractor driver who, as it happened, knew all about Raleigh Manor. She gave careful instructions and, as Harold turned to follow them, called, 'Watch your step.' She referred not to the boggy bit of Essex beneath his feet but to his destination.

Moss and Hazel trolled across the Common in search of a drink. They were celebrating the restoration of the door. This had been possible thanks to monies obtained from the Department of Health and Social Security and Moss's mother.

The Nightingale was packed.

Hazel spotted Walter clutching a half of bitter over by the cigarette machine.

'What'll it be, ladies?' cried the barperson.

Walter watched. Who was she with? A round soft fair girl, round face, round blue eyes. A girl who liked a laugh, you could tell. She was laughing now, raising a pink drink to pink lips.

Walter watched the bright blonde head dip toward the dark spikey one, watched the fat cheerful kiss planted on the pale waiting cheek. Pretty as a picture, he thought, draining his glass. Prettier, he thought.

Walter imagined himself ensconced in a large bed between them — silk sheets, all that. First they'd do things to each other while he watched. Then they'd do things to him while he instructed, and then he'd do things to them.

Should he go over and say hello to her, be introduced to her friend? But he was too late. By the time he'd imagined he'd made up his mind they'd gone.

Elvis stood on top of a pile of cardboard boxes, his nose pressed against the dark glass. Was he there?

Through cobwebs he saw the candle flame. He saw the dull gleam of the ice-cream scoop with the tangerine handle that, weeks ago, he'd stolen from the kitchen drawer. He saw the beloved Bogeyman tie a belt around his arm, dragging it tight with his teeth. He saw the small blister of liquid in the scoop, the needle's sipping spike.

Elvis sucked in his breath. The bit he liked best was coming next.

Moss often wondered why Harold had stopped phoning. She supposed he'd found another interest. She hoped he was happy now. *She* was: happy, as she and Hazel kissed under the street lamp by the railway bridge with its failed and faded exhortation to say 'NO TO CRUISE!!! and NO TO TRIDENT!!!' Soft rain falling on them in straight lines, soft tongues performing those mock cupulatory manoeuvres they both enjoyed so much. Happy.

Daphne looked up from her typewriter when Walter walked in. He kissed the top of her head.

'How is it?'

'Coming along.'

'Everything all right?'

'I think so. That woman thinks she can fix up Albert's stammer. She talked to him after school. He took to her, which is half the battle with him.'

Daphne switched off her typewriter, pushed back her chair and lit one of the five cigarettes lined up on the table in front of her.

'I wish you wouldn't.'

'I know.'

'I think I'll go and do the rounds.'

'You might ask Rupert what's in all those boxes in his room. He and that cross-eyed friend of his have been lugging them upstairs all evening. I did ask him, but he told me to fuck off, or words to that effect.'

'It's his age.'

'Is it, darling?' Daphne's eyes screwed up a little at the edges.

'He was the perfect child until he got pubic hair.'

'They all were.'

Moss peeped in on her own sweet sleeping boy and then went into the kitchen to make coffee to keep herself awake.

Hazel was already in bed, reading. Moss came in and clicked on the light above her workbench. Their happiness held. Moss settled down to work.

Soon the only sounds were her breathing, which tended to deepen as she concentrated, and the occasional scrape of turning pages against the bedcovers.

Moss was pleased with her layout for the Women Artists Calendar.

She looked across at Hazel. When Hazel was peaceful — usually when she was eating or reading — she looked about twelve years old. Moss loved her very much. She always had.

Angst, forgotten, drags a baby from its pram outside the fish and chip shop and does his best to eat it.

Harold had been nine when his father had prised up the floorboards and showed him the box of Belsen bits and pieces he kept hidden in the shed on the allotment.

He told Harold that he'd intended waiting until he was older before showing him these things but something had happened and he'd had to change his plans.

What was in this mossy box were things Harold's father had taken from various low-ranking guards when he'd been among the first Allied troops to enter Belsen. Mildewed photographs of sadistic sexual behaviour and pictures of the same tattooed on squares of skin. Also records of obscene medical experiments, a few wedding rings and what Harold had taken to be a leather pouch which proved to be an old ear.

Why had his father given him these things?

'So you'll know, son. So you'll know what people are all about under the surface.' And the next day he'd gone away.

'Gone for a soldier, dear' was what his mother had said he'd done but, after what his father had told him about being a soldier, Harold didn't think so.

Coming back from his early morning jog along the sea wall, Mozart vivid in his ears, le Professeur de Judo finds a familiar package propped against his apartment door.

It is the size and shape of a baby's coffin and bears a South London postmark. Order vanishes. Le Professeur tears off his headphones.

Mozart dies on the gaudy carpet of the corridor.

Inside the apartment Lucienne wakes, tunes in to her favourite FM station out of Seattle and, as luck would have it, hits on the ultimate classic killer sad song of all time and turns it up. The opening sob of the steel guitar lashes into her father's heart like a fish hook and lands him gasping on the ghastly carpet.

Bouncing on her bed, Lucienne sings along with Linda Ronstadt, unaware of the devastating chord structures of romantic sadness, oblivious to the tear-jerking power of the key of D.

> 'Oh and
> I've done everything I know
> To try and make you mine
> And I think it's gonna hurt me
> For a long long time . . .'

How long is that? How long exactly?
Le Professeur lies filleted on the floor.
The dread that the hurt won't ever end.
That 'a long long time' means forever.

Ted. Good God. Ted. What's brought this on? A full moon, pre-menstrual tension, what?

It was a hotel room. Late afternoon. Decades ago. Hot, as it often was then and in that place, and the phone failing to ring.

15

That morning she'd piled her wedding dress, veil and withered bouquet (for she'd not thrown it to anyone, not her) on top of the television as a sign of where his loyalties lay. And then she'd run away, leaving the phone number of this hotel so's he could ring her up and win her back.

It had been nice at first: eighteen-years-old, childish bride Hazel, lying reading *The Second Sex* on the bed, her feet in a patch of sunshine. But then he hadn't phoned. She'd pestered the reception desk for messages, gone for an agitated walk.

She'd switched on the television news, thinking to gain comfort in his absence by catching a glimpse of his work. But there had been no comfort in that blur of film, that image of fragility repeated in frames of glass, reflected on a blank background of faces, office workers gathered at their windows to watch the broken helicopter fluttering to earth between the towerblocks. It was remarkable, this film of a dedicated news cameraman doggedly recording his own end. It told her nothing she needed to know.

The small white fluted jug with violets painted on it that Moss was so fond of squeezed out of Hazel's squeaky grip and broke on the edge of the sink.

She gave a thin whine of dismay, raised her fat blue rubber-gloved hands to heaven and protested the discomfort and inconvenience of such mental indigestion, the chunks of the past bobbing rancid in her mind, causing her to chip, drop and fumble things.

The Women's Design Collective arrived for their meeting on foot, bike and rusty roller-skates.

'A loves B loves C loves D who has a vibrator,' whispered uncharitable Hazel, watching from an upstairs window.

A white Ford Cortina with multiple dents pulled up outside. Hazel wrapped her head in the curtains. She knew who this one was. It was the woman from Goondiwindi, who claimed she'd been at school with her. Yuk. It was a small world and all that.

Hazel had spent a long time inventing herself and didn't want any contradictory versions floating about. Even this one must have changed her name and habits. Hazel would surely remember being in the same class as a short red-headed baby-butch with Trotskyite tendencies called Buster. There hadn't been too many of those in Goondiwindi.

Hazel watched while whatsherface fussed about in the back of her car, fishing out a baby, which she strapped to her back before stamping up the front path, pulverising the gravel under her great big combat boots purchased in Fort Bragg, North Carolina. Moss had supplied this bit of information.

Moss had been besotted by this Buster person for a while. Hazel unwrapped her head and peered down at the baby. She had heard some funny stories about it: how they'd got it out of a yoghurt carton or something. In response to some bribe or other the milkman had jacked off into it and left it on the doorstep with the milk. Then her lover, Beulah, had impregnated Buster with a disposable plastic syringe while they made love on the floor.

In fact Hazel didn't know where, how, or even if, the deed had taken place, but somehow she saw it happening on the floor.

The front door slammed behind Buster and the baby.

Hazel's foot had gone to sleep. She stamped around the room a bit and decided to go out and find Walter.

She'd heard some horror story about a mad dog when she'd been queueing up to cash her supplementary benefit giro down at the post-office that morning. Now the police had come into it.

Walter saw her coming: saw her high-heeled boots dancing down the frosty pavement, the calculated swirl of her raincoat swinging open to reveal a tartan lining, her quick grin as she saw him sitting in the steamed-up window of the cafe opposite the Old People's Home in Northcote Road.

In she came. She shed her raincoat, revealing tight pencil-leg jeans and a black and gold jumper, out at the elbow, left over from the Biba days. She pulled out a chair and plumped down beside him.

'Well?' she demanded.

She's got a super bum, he thought. He allowed himself a quick glimpse of her bent over in front of him, her jeans and knickers round her knees, her hands gripping the far edge of the wonky formica table as he reared over her, preparing to enter from behind.

'Why not?' cried Hazel to the frazzled woman gesturing at her from behind the espresso machine. And to Walter, 'What're you going to do about it?'

'Do?'

'About your dog.'

'Ssh,' yelped Walter, smacking a hand over his own mouth, though it was her he'd dearly like to throttle.

'I could help you look for it.'

'I've looked.'

'We'll look again.'

Walter cheered up a bit. A trouble shared was a trouble halved, as it were. The children were out of the question. Daphne didn't bear thinking about. The police were bloody hopeless. As usual, it was all up to him.

Hazel's eyes stared frankly at him over her coffee cup.

'You will let me help you, won't you?'

'Why not,' said Walter, feeling much better. 'This is very good of you.'

What was that look on her face? That half smile. What was it? It reminded him of something, of someone. He gave it up. After all, it could hardly matter.

Hazel advanced her hand toward his across the table. A pause before Walter laughed, rose to his feet and jammed her hand against the front of his trousers so that she would feel his erection. Hazel did not take her hand away. Nor did she make any remark.

The frazzled woman did. She promised them the old heave-ho if they didn't pack it in. So they left.

Le Professeur de Judo and his wife Hazel leave the General Hospital where their child, the Little Lucienne, has been rushed earlier that night to have her appendix out. She lies quiet now, peaceful and without pain, while her parents whirl across the parking lot through big wet snowflakes which land and glisten in their hair: pretty crowns for those light-headed with relief.

They find that the lock on their car has frozen and will not take the key. Le Professeur de Judo unzips his fly, piddles on the handle and melts the lock, sticking his key in quick before the thing can change its mind. Now they are ready to go home, but not quite, for Hazel stays his hand as it fumbles to put himself away before his prick turns blue and drops off to lie in the snowy lot like a rude popsicle.

She wants him, she says. Here, now, as she lies on her back across the frosty hood, and pulls him over her like a rug.

'Bear,' she says. 'My great big bear.'

And afterwards when he's fallen out and regained his feet she's still sprawled there with a fine condensation rising from between her open legs in clouds like breath-frost hanging on the cold night air, or dry ice rising from a trap-door in some poorly staged pantomine in a small mad town far away, for this and other images go dancing through her head as he's taken her hands and pulled her to her feet. The back of her leather jacket makes stuck and tearing sounds as it peels away from the frozen metal, and he's afraid the same will happen to the skin on her bottom but she comes away quite easily, leaving nothing of herself behind, and stands laughing in his arms, so weak with it in fact that he has to pull up her soft black corduroy trousers himself and fold her to him to muffle the noise lest the attendant nodding over the *National Enquirer* in her brightly lit glass booth looks up and is forced to draw their attention to a sign which reads SILENCE: YOU ARE IN A HOSPITAL ZONE.

That same hotel. The one in Sydney.

The management broke their way in, alerted by sounds of pain and confusion drifting under the door and echoing dully down the dusty corridor. They found her trying to do a perish with a bit of blunt razor-blade, babbling of love.

'I'll never find out,' Hazel confided to the policewoman who was patching her up. 'I'll never know.'

'Well, we none of us know — do we, dear? Not when you come right down to it. It's all a matter of faith.' This woman had spent a lot of time talking lunatics out of their tight corners. 'Faith, hope and charity, these three. Just think of that before you ever try such a silly thing again.'

'And love,' adds Hazel hopefully.

'If you like,' says the policewoman.

When things are sorted out, the television company sends the widowed Hazel a fat compensation cheque in the mail. She cashes it quick before they change their minds, takes a course in shorthand and typing, gasses the cat and sets out to see the world.

It was a gorgeous evening. The sun, setting beyond the distant towerblocks, slowly glazed the sky to glory. Winter seemed on the verge of softening into spring, the sky above Battersea Rise washed with lavender.

Moss sat on the roof, omniscient and dreamy, one arm round the chimney pot. She'd checked the guttering. It seemed OK. She'd cleaned out the dead leaves, an empty Silk Cut packet (Harold's?) and rubbish dropped by passing birds.

The hard physical work of moving the heavy extension ladder around the house, of climbing up and down, had cleared her mind of the babble of that morning's meeting and she hoped she'd be able to work tonight.

Moss was often exhausted by the battle to work as she wished, remain politically correct and deal with the droves of dick-heads (Hazel's phrase: Hazel was no help) who got in the way.

That bloody Beulah, for example, breaking in on the meeting like that: making speeches, upsetting Manny, Maureen and Sue, confiscating Elvis's Barbie doll on the grounds that it encouraged the stereotype of affluent, able-bodied, white and ultra-thin females, and complaining when he bit her and Moss made her give it him back.

Who was she, anyway? Some kind of sixties culture star from the Bowery and the Bellevue (electric shock treatment, ravishment, rats) who'd hung in there nonetheless. Who'd fucked Kate Millett — or was it Jill Johnston — or possibly both. The information was sketchy, supplied by the breathless and adoring Buster.

Moss bit her lip. Perhaps she was being unfair. Perhaps she was jealous. Perhaps she still fancied the now noisily monogamous Buster.

Moss watched Mr and Mrs Fisher next door, lured outside after their supper by the surprising weather.

Moss knew that if she put herself out she could still have Buster: on occasional afternoons, for example.

Mr Fisher oiled the lawnmower. Mrs Fisher forked over the edges of her compost heap.

But the point was — was Moss, at her age (forty-three), prepared to flounder her way through yet another hot and hopeless romance? She rather thought not.

Mrs Fisher turned a suspicious face to heaven — the face of one who knows her luck can't hold — saw Moss and shook her fist. Moss smiled, waved and called good evening and nice weather for the time of year. Mr Fisher poked out his tongue. Moss sighed. Acceptance was hard to come by.

A darkling plain.

Two monstrous figures, armed with axes, circle each other, armour clad.

The great black plumes on their helmets sweep the heavens like brooms, tumbling the stars, the planets and all such points of reference.

The axes open vast and silent wounds.

Outside, the persistent rain of the Pacific North West gentles the traffic noise to a soothing swish.

Le Professeur opens his eyes.

He has seen the final loneliness that beckons and yammers at the edges of his life.

He must do something.

Next morning Moss opened her eyes and knew, without stirring, that the world had changed overnight. The cottonwool quiet alerted her. Bright light blared round the edges of the curtains. Moss rattled them back on their tortoiseshell rings. Snow: robust and creamy heaps of it, glaring in the sun, blue and delicate between the houses where the sun was slow to penetrate: another planet. It was: a whole new world, with all that was not pleasing buried — including that rusty cooker flat on its back in the middle of the road which they'd been waiting decades for the bloody council to collect.

The bald and sticky privet next door was a gorgeous glittering riot.

The diamante skeleton of a pair of underpants, caught high in winter branches of the tree outside their bedroom, twinkled at Moss as she banged on the glass, forcing the window open and sticking her head out in a dislodged flurry of snow.

A big bad wolf frolicked in the garden below, plucking up her son and tossing him skywards screaming with glee, howling with laughter as he tumbled down into the featherbed of snow. The camera. Where was the camera? She wanted to have it forever, this picture of her boy, her beautiful boy brighter than a thousand buttons and her lover beaming and bear-like in that astonishing Eskimo suit she'd picked up somewhere on her travels, with its fantastical pointed hood, with dog-fur trim, that took up so much space in the wardrobe.

Moss found her camera, kissed it for still containing film, put on all the clothes she could find and dashed down to join them.

Angst cringed and shivered against the Bogeyman. Oh shit, thought the Bogeyman. I'm going to die. The dog too. This fucking dog is going to die.

He had his moments of lucidity.

This was a respite: this would ground the dog. Daphne joined him at the window.

'Extraordinary. Imagine the mess when it melts,' she said, thinking of old people popping out like snowdrops to break their bones on treacherous pavements.

'The children love it.'

Walter wanted to take the two youngest (Albert and Felicity) on to the Common this afternoon to build a snowman.

'Do we have any old carrots?' he asked, thinking of noses. He'd ask the others to come, of course, but doubted they'd accept. Benjamin, Felix and Dominic preferred the company of their friends. And Rupert — out of nowhere sprang an unhappy vision of his wild and vulpine eldest son, lost and snarling, unreachable in the snowy dark.

Walter resisted his impulse to run upstairs and check.

He knew Rupert was at home. Had heard him clumping up the stairs past his parents' room.

'Goodnight, old chap,' he had called, though it was more like dawn, and had received no reply as the boy stomped on up to the lair he'd made in the attic.

Rupert's unbending desperado despair and ultimately lonely attitudes touched his father's heart.

Why was he like this? What reason could there be? His babyhood planned and protected: his first books monitored — cats in hats, rats in spats: and nothing unduly Grimm. Pleasant pictures on his nursery walls — on every wall in the house for that matter — and no bloody television.

Walter shrugged on his coat and shivered.

Daphne was in the corner, burning toast.

Rupert's pretensions of thuggery were taking on political overtones. Walter had found no boxes in his room that night (why not — where had they gone?) and no Rupert either; but he had found three different bomb recipes, a stack of pro-IRA leaflets and, on his outgrown schoolboy desk, with its inky map of the world glued to the top, an unfinished letter beginning:

> Dear Colonel Ghadafi,
> I am fifteen years old and very strong.
> I work with weights every day. If you
> ever need help you can count on me. I
> have taken what our German colleagues
> call 'der sprung'. There is no going
> back. In Karl Heinzens' immortal words,
> 'Even if you have to blow up half a
> continent, have no qualms'.
>
> P.T.O.

Walter had turned the paper over, but there was nothing on the back.

Walter jammed on his hat. He'd walk to work — another respite. They'd all use the snow as an excuse not to turn up today. He'd get some work done without his staff to hinder him.

'Can I c-c-c-come?'

Albert sat on a tea-tray at the top of the steps which rose out of Daphne's garden to the front gate set in a stone wall. Snow had filled the garden to the top of the sundial and turned the steps into a small toboggan run.

Walter picked him up and swung him onto his shoulder, and they tramped off up the street.

Daphne watched them go. Like Tiny Tim and whatsit, she thought. Daphne knew that Walter often wondered why, and felt quite sorry for him. She didn't wonder much. She recorded what she knew of an inimical world, gave it a twist of her own and spat it out. As she hardly ever went out, she had a certain glum innocence which, thanks mostly to Walter, she was able to keep intact. Walter did not like his wife's books, though he admired their first-strike prose: 'short novels in which large and awful events are seen as continuous with the batterings of everyday life' (*Times Lit. Sup.*).

Harold had come to regard the box as an inheritance. In time he'd grown to value the photographs over the rest. Realising that these would fit nicely into a manila envelope easily purchased at any W. H. Smith, and would be a good deal easier to conceal than his father's box, this is what he'd done. Then he set about ridding himself of the box and its remaining contents.

Thinking to put it back where it came from, he got on his bike and rode to the allotments. The shed had been razed, and in its place stood a greenhouse in which grew ranks of unpleasant waxy flowers shaped the way girls were underneath. Harold wondered what to do. He walked along newly laid gravel paths that scrunched under his feet like mouthfuls of marbles, setting his teeth on edge. He walked past the fence at the back. He picked up a stick and knocked down weeds, looking for a loose paling.

Finding one, he pulled it aside and stepped through onto the tow-path at the edge of the Grand Union Canal. The poxy facades of the decaying terraces on the opposite bank shuddered as trains passed on the railway lines behind them. Harold clutched his box and stood looking at the black water as it oozed along so slowly that at first Harold had thought it still, until the progress of a sack wriggling its way downstream between the rusted girders of the road bridge to Harold's left and a snarl of brambles rearing over the water with its roots in the rubble to his right showed him otherwise. At this point the wriggling sack thrashed about and sank. This seemed an excellent place to rid himself of the box. He threw it into the middle of the canal. It skidded across the oily surface and sank. A slow stream of dirty bubbles rose to the top like farts in a bath.

Moss and Hazel quarrelled. And the day had begun so promisingly too, with the frolic in the garden and mulled wine for breakfast (boiled egg and milky tea for Elvis).

Hazel had prepared the wine. Its fragrance filled the kitchen, and Hazel had looked so imposing — so unlikely: sipping, talking, laughing, kicking her legs like a kid on a jetty as she sat on the kitchen window-ledge — that Moss had simply rolled on the floor with glee.

Sun shone on Hazel's fur as she leaned over Moss, caressing the pale sweet skin of her neck, raising her jumper and grazing her nipples with her teeth. Hazel was about to slide her hand down inside Moss's old grey corduroy trousers when they heard Elvis coming.

'Later,' promised Hazel.

Moss laughed and went to get another bottle out of the wardrobe on the first-floor landing.

After breakfast they had gone up to the Common.

Hazel had read a book once, set in some olden time when snow had fallen on London and the Thames had frozen and people had skated up and down on ice so thick it had been possible to light fires on it. She'd often pictured that, and now here it was — sort of. The pond was packed with people falling about.

Hazel happily supplied the flames. Beyond them blurred Beulah, over by the park-keeper's hut. Hazel focussed her eyes. It was her, all right, blazing an amorous trail through the snow, video pack strapped to her back, taping Buster as she guided the baby through its first snow experience.

Moss moaned. The warmth of the second bottle of Sainsbury's Vin du Pays l'Ardenne was wearing off. The jolly Common stretched before her, weary as the wastes of Russia. Her left sock kept slipping down inside her wellington no matter how she tugged it. It was irritating, when all she wanted to think about was going back to bed with Hazel this afternoon. They'd smoke some of those nice old hippie drugs she still kept stashed around the place to cheer her, and finish what they'd started.

It didn't work out that way. The trouble began during a game of Happy Families.

Elvis, frustrated because he couldn't find family-members to go with Primrose the Peace Campaigner or Carole the Councillor, tore Garry the Gay in half. Moss sent him to his room for being a bad sport.

Once there Elvis climbed out of the window, slid down the drainpipe, nicked round the back of the house to the kitchen, picked up a jar of Grandma's strawberry jam and hot-footed it to the Bogeyman's.

Hazel drew a moustache on Poppy the Plumber. She didn't want to play this game any more. Moss took the crayon away. Hazel snatched it back. It broke. Hazel chucked both bits at Moss. Each piece struck an eye, causing tears. Moss covered them with her hands. From behind this barrier she told Hazel that she should grow up.

'I can't.'

And that was the truth. There is more, but she knows she must not say it: that she feels cut off from, and has no enthusiasm for, the world. She is afraid. She cannot escape from the evil of hopelessness. It's a pity, but there it is.

'Being human is the condition of being deathbound and sexed.' Who'd said that? Mum? His English teacher? Jesus? Or the dirty man who talked to himself on the bus all the time?

Whoever'd said it, Harold was sure he was it personified as he entered his teenage years all mad and obsessed. What was wrong? Wasn't his Mum feeding him right? It was true that his first wet dreams span round a centrepiece of himself garrotting a fellow-prisoner and stealing his half-eaten potato, but nutrition wasn't the problem.

Each night after his tea Harold went to his room and wandered his landscape of the dead. Dachau, Auschwitz, Treblinka — he tried them all, but back he came, back back back to Bergen-Belsen.

Elvis's tears splash sad and hot onto the Bogeyman's eyelids and thaw them. He shoves urgent fingers thick with strawberry jam between this creep's grey lips. The Bogeyman widens the slits of his chipped junkie eyes.

'Please, please,' Elvis whispers, though he has no idea what it is he pleads for.

A dim image forms on the fried cheese surface of the Bogeyman's retina. He has an idea but loses it. He closes his eyes. Elvis blubbers. The Bogeyman hisses weakly, grabs the child's wrist, snares it in a tight circlet of bone while he tracks his idea through his smashed and cratered brain.

He has it — yes — nails it hard to the back of his skull and examines it. Much as he intends to nail Elvis to the cellar wall. Later: when he has the strength. Because kids can be useful — right?

The Bogeyman laughs (sort of).

Elvis laughs.

The Bogeyman will take Elvis out into suburban streets every afternoon and shove him through letter-boxes to steal things: video cassette recorders — something like that. The exhausted Bogeyman licks up the jam and sleeps.

Elvis creeps away.

He loves the Bogeyman and would like to stay and watch over him. But he loves his mother too and does not wish to worry her. The very thought causes something long, dark, slippery and filled

27

with teeth to nudge his elbow. What's that? Elvis hurries up.

Soon pain will wake the Bogeyman. The shock and force of it will shake his idea loose.

But, as his health and the weather improves, so will his memory.

She'd spent the winter of her twenty-ninth year in New York.

It had been a time of hard work and personal loss, and when it had ended she'd found herself with enough money to buy a car.

She bought an Alfa Romeo Sprint.

She'd driven it across the country in a crazy state of mind. She'd told herself stories, mixing past and present at random, in love with her own stubborn sadness.

She'd had some thought of dying, but no plan she could put her finger on.

She'd stopped as seldom as possible.

Martha. Eighteen years old. From Lake Woebegone, Saskatchewan. Martha lies on her back under a dead Christmas tree nobody knows how to get rid of, doing tricky things with her vaginal muscles.

Le Professeur redoubles his efforts, thrusting harder to show how much he appreciates the efforts of his prettiest pupil. And then, just as his labours might form themselves into passion, his elbow slips on a ribbon-trimmed package (for her cousin in California, which she had forgotten to post), jarring his funny-bone and bringing him straight back to his senses.

He slips away from her and lies wondering at his folly, as the room fills with the doomy notes of the song of the humped-back whale that he's triggered off through the bright paper.

He stares at her and knows that not only has he done her harm, he has done himself no good at all.

'But I have saved this afternoon for you,' she whispers. 'Saved it for you. Made excuses, arrangements, emptied the apartment with obvious lies, pleading a need to be alone, and now you've gone and spoilt it.' He has spoilt it: he has and knows it. Yet he appears not to be listening and sits silently digging the carpet fluff from his fingernails with a pine needle.

'I have to go.'

'Oh surely not,' she moans. 'Not now. Come on. There's still time.'

She nuzzles his shoulder, winds her arms round his neck to topple him. He rocks like a round plastic toy in the bottom of a budgie cage.

He sees his face mad and gloomy in a blue glass bauble. Shreds of tinsel shimmer along the dark hairs of his forearm.

He steadies himself, gropes under an armchair for his shoes and socks. She squeals in protest, wraps her legs round his waist and rides on his back. They sway about the room like some nightmarishly erotic Indian sculpture sprung to life.

'Two hours,' he pleads. 'On the phone you said two hours only.'

The front door slams. 'There you are,' he hisses. 'They're back.'

'It's all right,' she soothes. 'They won't come in, not while the door's shut.'

Nonetheless she falls away from him. He dresses. He longs to say something to her — that this ghastly masquerade has been his mistake, that he would like to be friends — but he has used her enough. He leaves.

And now that she is free to do so his prettiest ex-pupil weeps. She thinks she will go home. She thinks she will drive her father's dog-team across frozen Lake Woebegone, carve up a patch of wilderness, build a log-cabin, hang out with bears.

In the event, what she does is fly to New York with a girl-friend, see lots of shows and slowly start to feel better.

Sixteen years old and unable to bear it, Harold had burned his photographs, eyes stinging with smoke and tears because in doing so he felt he was betraying his father but, at that point, he felt it was him or him, or every man for himself, or something like that because he couldn't sort out his thoughts. He'd run outside into the street, clung weeping to a lamp-post while the wind whipped leaves and stuff round his trouser legs, and the images all came back and he knew that even if he tore his eyes out and flung them in the gutter he'd still not be rid of the pictures, because they were printed deep in his head in a place he couldn't get at except, perhaps, with a hatchet.

'I had a Godmother once who said to me, "If you go through life looking for the worst in people, you're bound to find it."'

'Where is she?'

'Where's who?'

'This Godmother you had once.'

Moss, whom no one had thought to provide with a Godmother, blushed.

'Liar! Liar! Your pants are on fire!' crowed Elvis.

'Leave it out,' said Moss and Hazel together. Moss smiled. Hazel smiled back. Perhaps it will be all right, thought Moss, perhaps it will. Perhaps all we need is a holiday — quite a long one — so that when we get back things will have cheered up. Moss's mind played with various ways and means by which they could afford it.

'Listen,' commanded Hazel. '"The ultimate goal is release from rebirth and suffering: extinction. To be cremated in Benares and to have one's ashes sprinkled upon the holy Ganges ensures this liberation".'

'Where did you find that?'

'In a sack in the cellar.'

Moss thought she'd dumped all that old junk of Harold's. Apparently not.

'The thing is,' murmured Moss, more or less to herself, 'that it shouldn't be that difficult. I fully expect to gain extinction when I die without lifting a finger.'

'I think there's more to it than extinction,' said Hazel, frowning at a coloured illustration of a short fat man with an elephant's head seated on a rat.

'I daresay there is,' said Moss and went on with her ironing.

Elvis went on building his Lego castle. 'Dungeons,' he whispered, 'and angels.'

Nicholas jumped on Hazel's lap and yawned.

'Dragons,' corrected Moss.

'Angels,' insisted Elvis.

'This cat has filthy breath,' remarked Hazel.

'Yes. Well,' said Moss, looking up from her best silk blouse and stretching out her hand to ruffle the top of Hazel's anxious, spikey hair.

Moss went back to her ironing and Hazel went back to the beginning. She had no trouble conjuring them up: a small Moss, a smaller Hazel, comfortably curled on the back seat of Hazel's Dad's brand new Ford Prefect motor-car where Moss is kissing Hazel's cherry pink knees. The thick black coil of the garden hose may barely be seen, hanging on a nail behind a door which slowly opens.

Hazel notes with sobbing affection how, in the bright stabs of her mother's torch, Moss has a filmy beading of sweat between her eyebrows.

Then the travelling had begun: foreign parts, her mother's tears and inconsolable homesicknesses — all Hazel's fault. Even though she hadn't let Moss pull her knickers down. Years later she'd realised that it wasn't — that she'd had nothing to do with it at all.

It had been a warm evening. Nothing on television had been worth watching and Harold had been out, so his mother had drawn herself a cool bath and lain in it listening to the sounds of her empty house, the distant traffic, the muffled clip-clop of horses from the Cavalry Barracks taking their evening exercise, while her mind drifted, dipping, peaceful down the beach.

Mrs Birtwhistle had closed her eyes and smiled to see sunlight breaking in colours on waves that fell at her feet, colours she'd never forgotten nor tried to name, but simply taken out from time to time to play with. A happy childhood, she'd thought, is a priceless treasure. She'd hoped Harold had had one, but common sense said not. The times had been against it.

She'd hoped he was out with a girl. She'd decided he was and was pleased. Thinking idly of love and other related matters, she'd stroked her fingers across her breasts, gently squeezing, and there it was, the lump. Not even that: the tiniest thing, rolling beneath her fingers like a pea dipped in grease.

Mrs Birtwhistle was not one to give up easily. She'd tried everything medical science had had to offer, but it did no good, and in the end, in a condition far worse than that in which she'd started out, Harold's mother had come home to die.

Those men from the Council whose job it was to comb the Borough's derelict buildings for corpses hadn't given much for their chances when they'd found Angst and the Bogeyman stuck together with frost.

But you can't keep a good man down. At least that's what the psychiatric social worker up at the hospital told Eric, which is what the Bogeyman had said his name was.

The psychiatric social worker and all the nurses had a lot of time for Eric, because the first words he'd uttered when he came round were about a dog. A man like that couldn't be all bad.

Angst stayed with the RSPCA until Eric was well enough to claim him. The staff there had grown quite fond of him and christened him Max. They'd also had him seen to, which quietened Max down a bit.

When the time came, the psychiatric social worker drove Eric to the RSPCA to pick up Max, and then drove them to the half-way house he'd managed to find that would take them both.

All Eric had to do now was to pop in for a chat with the psychiatric social worker once a week.

Following a defile, the road descends rapidly for 2,000 feet to bring Hazel to a sheet of green water which breaks across her eyes like the ocean. Warm breezes ruffle its surface. Pelicans bob on curls of turquoise. Blind fish hang suspended in its depths, fat as zeppelins, blunt as thumbs. Hazel removes her clothes, enters the water (slightly saline) and starts to swim toward the remarkable rock formation that rises in the lake's centre and gives the place its name.

Located thirty miles north-east of Reno, Nevada, accessible only by crossing the diminished lands of the Paiute Indian nation,

Pyramid Lake is approximately 25 miles long, four to 11 miles wide and more than 300 feet deep.

'Sit on my face,' invited the mad old black lady in the woolly Rastafarian hat who lived under the bench at the launderette with only a coloured picture of Princess Di for company.

Hazel sighed. All domestic chores fell to her these days, while Moss worked to finish the calendar ahead of deadline so they could go on holiday.

Where is Elvis? He was here a second ago.

Hazel stepped over the black lady's bandaged legs and went to the door to look. No sign of Elvis in the street. Instead there is Beulah, Buster (no baby) and Manny staggering down the street under a load of film-making equipment.

'No peace for the wicked,' observed the mad old black lady. *She* should know. They'd been after her for weeks.

Beulah had made the Greater London Council Women's Committee give them money to do it.

Their quarry shot back under her bench. Beulah shot in after her. Buster and Manny set up. Hazel stood about, wishing the washing was done. There were sounds of struggle from under the bench.

'What am I?' asked the mad old black lady.

'You are a woman of colour. That is the favoured term since the word "black" excludes so many and may in itself be considered elitist and therefore discriminatory,' explained Beulah.

Hazel went to the door. Where was Elvis? Buster followed.

'You sat next to me at school until Miss Hughes split us up. She said you were a bad influence. You wrote me notes and made me laugh.'

'Sit on my face,' bellowed the mad old woman of colour.

'Sure! Why not?' said the intrepid Beulah. If Arbus had slept with all sorts of scabby dwarfs and weirdos to get her pictures — well then, she could too.

Hazel blinked. Did I? But the past is another country. Didn't someone say that? She felt sick. She honestly did. The walls marched towards her. Buster grabbed her arm, sat her on the bench. Hazel hoped she wasn't going to cry, but she was. Manny handed her a big blue handkerchief. Beulah stuck her head out.

'What're you crying for — the plight of women living lives as defined by the patriarchy?' Beulah wiggled out, hauling the mad old black woman with her and shaking her for emphasis. 'Or are you just another female neurotic, only too happy to be very sad in the old style? D'you know what I see when I look at you?'

Hazel didn't.

'Well, I get this flash, you know — this image of a woman forever looking out of windows: a woman existing at one remove from life itself with a head full of roses, fairy-tales and fucking — a Madame Bovary type.'

Hazel thought of making a dash for it. There was no law that said she had to sit and listen to this. On the other hand, Beulah was talking about her, which was always interesting. But now Beulah was bringing Moss into it — about how she and Hazel were so heavily into this whole personal drama of what they liked to think of as being their unique, secret and impossible relationship that the political shit coming down around them touched them not at all.

'All you want is this happy, hassle-free life,' accused Beulah. 'Right? Am I right?' Beulah slapped her forehead with the flat of her hand to order her thoughts before continuing. She strutted a few steps and struck a braggadocio pose over by the extractor.

Hazel thought she looked terrific. She felt that faint ache of sexual attraction she usually felt for bullies. Hazel was so irritated by this that she missed the first bit of what Beulah was saying.

What she did hear was how she and Moss were acting out this old romantic dyke-type life led along dead literary lines: exclusive, full of high sentiment like Gertrude and Alice, Radclyffe and Una, Djuna and . . . Djuna and?

'Thelma,' supplied Manny, crawling across the floor with a fistful of cables looking for a powerpoint.

'All the great dead dykes,' sneered Beulah. 'Serves them right.' What? What does, or, rather, did — wondered Hazel.

Beulah closed in. Beulah wanted Hazel to know that she, Beulah, held her personally responsible for Moss's growing neglect of the Collective and for her increasing tendency to

34

confuse personal anecdote with political analysis.

Hazel hummed, asking herself how much longer she'd have to put up with this.

Approximately ten seconds, as it happened, because this was when, weakened by all the weird weather, the pipes burst. Water gushed out from under the machines, overtaking Manny as she bent to plug in her cables. A shriek. A shower of sparks and darkness.

Hazel took advantage of the chaos and slipped away. She'd retrieve her washing in the dead of night, if it hadn't all gone down the drain, or been nicked.

Elvis sniffed the stained mattress. Dog hairs stuck to his nose. Where had the Bogeyman gone? Had he gone the way of all Daddies? Elvis didn't know, but he felt very, very sad.

A long way back. Before Ted had come to town to cover some drought, flood, or bushfire, or possibly all three. Further than she wants to go tonight or ever. Fuck 'Buster'. Hazel had put two and two together. Hazel remembered Julie: giggly, her hair not red at all but more the colour of buried bones. There must be more. 'Buster' hadn't seemed so short at the time. It's just that she hadn't grown much since.

Buster and Beulah had a long talk about Hazel while they ate their supper. They analysed her dodgy past and peculiar attitudes. Buster was more interested in these things than Beulah, though Beulah was curious about Australians because of the films that came from there, cast up at the local Odeon like letters in a bottle.

Afterwards Beulah had some paperwork to do and did it. Buster couldn't settle to anything. So she wrote Moss a letter. She walked around to the house and slid it under the door. In it were lots of things that Moss ought to know about Hazel's background. Buster felt a bit ashamed of herself afterwards. And so she should have.

Walter hadn't seen Hazel for ages. Just as well. He thought of his wife's large, restless, rather unforgiving eyes. He'd been right about the dog too. No sign of it. And business was all right. What more could he want? What he wanted was a heart-to-heart with Rupert, but the boy avoided him.

Like eighteen-year-old Martha from Saskatchewan, twelve-year-old Johny Holy Joy from Streatham didn't come into it much really. He'd been Rupert's sidekick. Not a friend. Rupert didn't admit of friends. None the less Johny had gone to his house that night around seven o'clock and they'd rummaged about a bit and had no bother coming up with the twelve quid they'd needed for a gram of amphetamine sulphate plus the bus fare to Finsbury Park to get it. Johny intended saving his share for the weekend. Not so Rupert. By the time they got over to Archway he'd been flying.

'As though some magic lantern through the nerves like patterns on a screen,' he cried, poised on the platform of a No. 27 bus, sucking on the bottle of Scotch they'd taken from Walter's desk and mangling his favourite poet. The conductor wouldn't come near him. Rupert jumped off as they passed the station.

Little Johny had tumbled after, scarcely able to think, so anxious about everything was he. He wasn't supposed to come over here, not on a school night, but here he was and there was that mad fucker Rupert leading him on rubber legs up a narrow iron ladder crusted with soot and pulling away from the wall in places as they climbed.

Rupert never closed his gob. Bits of words showered down on Johny as he followed the faint gleam of Rupert's studded boot-heels up to the roof. Rupert was clever, as everyone agreed: a quick thinker. He had to have the last word.

'Nuke it now,' he'd found time to scream as, stepping clear of the ladder, he'd slipped and crashed through the roof of Archway station, still clutching his father's bottle of J&B.

Mrs Birtwhistle lay still on the fresh white sheet stretched taut beneath her. Harold stuffed the old soiled one in a plastic bag and checked that he had change for the launderette.

Harold had had to take leave from his job at the Government Printing Office in Hackney. Everyone had been very understanding. They didn't know he wanted flogging and locking up.

'Are you cold?'

She didn't answer. She didn't want to be covered, couldn't bear the weight of the lightest blanket. She was bald and had no flesh left. She was starving yet couldn't eat, in pain but frightened to die. Looking at her, Harold had to bend forward slightly to hide his erection.

'To cease upon the midnight with no pain.' What idiot had written that? Someone who didn't know his arse from his elbow. Someone who hadn't seen the newsreels, someone whose father had failed to provide them with photographs. Or possibly nobody at all. Harold was hopeless at quotes, making them up or twisting them round to suit himself. He felt cursed and wicked, and yet he did his best — but, just as he'd always known it wouldn't be, his best wasn't good enough. He hadn't even been there when she'd died. He'd been round the corner at the off-licence buying half a bottle of brandy.

He'd sat a good while on the floor by her bed, his eyes filled with dying children and hopeless parents, his ears filled with the merry hiss of gas from the waiting showers.

He'd taken his half-bottle of brandy and poured a few drops into each of her excavated armpits. He'd trickled more onto her chest, watched it travel along the runnels of her scars and flood the concavity which had been his mother's belly. He'd licked it off and wondered what, if any, solitary crime he was committing. He'd been saved the misery of further invention when sleep slipped a big black bag over his head.

They'd all been very furtive at the funeral, all those old relatives, amazed that they'd outlived her.

'A good boy . . . .,' 'a loving son . . . .,' 'a rare bird and makes a lovely sandwich . . . .', And other murmurs along those lines had circulated through the house after the cremation, along with the tea and buns and the sherry for those who needed it.

What would they have done if Harold had tapped his teaspoon

on the rim of his teacup for silence and, having obtained it, told them all what it really meant — this noble nursing of his mother through her final months — told them what he'd done? Would they natter and judge? Would their dentures tumble down upon the carpet? Would they fall on him with old raucous cries and gum him to death?

One night in the Mid-West, when a hunters' moon hung huge, low and possibly magical, in that it wore a witch's hat of cloud, and she'd been driving thirty-two hours straight with the assistance of chemical additives — well, anyway, sometime that night, and without taking her eyes from Interstate 12, she'd ejected Bruce Springsteen and fed the first cassette her hand fell on into the slot and such purely glorious music had filled the car — the recitative and duet from the first act of *Lakmé*— that her heart had swelled like the moon with forgiveness and exhaustion, and an old and lonely wish that, if only Lark were here to share it, the music would sound even better and everything would be all right.

So she'd stopped at a booth somewhere and put through a call.

Steven had picked up the phone.

Lark, he said, was safe asleep.

Safe from her.

Her importuning and insults.

Her insistent pitting of passion against domesticity.

Saved by him from all those months of their working and, sometimes, out of town, in other States of the Union, sleeping together in rooms above drained swimming pools filled with dead leaves chattering in the wind and the moaning of the ripped up clouds and Lark moaning too, under her tongue. Under her thumb.

Steven told her that he was in the bath, working on some papers. She remembered Steven had some kind of back trouble. She forgot exactly what.

Was Lark there?

Had she picked up the bedroom extension?

Hazel could see the moonlight spilling through the great cathedral windows of the loft, saw that view clear across the Hudson which thousands would kill for.

Was Lark there, that quick light breathing on the line — was that her or the prairie wind throbbing in the wire?

And then, splashing the water for emphasis, 'Please don't call us any more because we don't enjoy this any more than you do.'

Why him?

Why not me?

Steven's slender purple penis floated on the surface of the water, borne up by bubbles, peaceful as lugworm bait.

She fought the stupid door of the booth to get out.

Some sensation of internal tearing indicated that she was vomiting up her heart. It broke like an egg on the road's black surface and splashed her neat white leather running shoes. She stepped round her heart to the car. She drove away, putting her foot down, laying some rubber because, whether you are in love or any other type of trouble, you are in it less at 120 miles per hour.

She stood in the shadows watching his windows until the last light went out. It was late when she walked away to find a phone box from which to call a mini-cab.

Had Hazel watched a bit longer she might have heard the phone ring in Walter's basement kitchen, would certainly have seen first one and then all the lights blaze back, would even perhaps have heard the cry that rose through all three storeys to fray and fade like smoke against the night sky.

But instead she waited round the corner, thinking mainly of Moss while the moon slid swiftly down until it clung, a grubby blister on the fleeing heel of night, somewhere to the right of Battersea Rise. A new day. A new leaf. Hazel vowed to turn it.

As she did every Sunday at 6.30, Moss telephoned her mother in Bournemouth.

Yes, she'd adore to have Elvis for a while provided she could call him David.

Moss put him on the train, keeping her fingers crossed that he'd not set light to anything. She needn't have worried. David wouldn't dream of doing such a thing. He loved to visit his

Grandma's house. In particular he loved the high-ceilinged, silent sitting-room with hundreds of tiny glass animals on every flat surface and the grandfather clock in the hall which gave the house its steady heartbeat.

He enjoyed the afternoon walk they always took with the dachsie, down through the winding chines to the promenade, where they left Fritz to roam like a restless turd round the floral clock, while they went to their favourite tea-room.

The best part though, despite the cakes and so on, was coming back in the late afternoon, when he'd race ahead to open the front door, turn off the burglar alarm and run down the hall to the room where the creatures all waited dull with dusk for the moment he'd switch on the wall lamps. Then what an intricate shimmer of whispers would ring out as the room turned shiny and snug and Granny swept in, saying, 'Time for a sherry, I think,' as though there were ever any doubt about that, or anything else in the world for that matter, and all the sharp whispering ceased.

Later he'd go upstairs to sleep in Mummy's old bed surrounded by the things he supposed she didn't want any more.

One night in this room Elvis dreamed a terrible dream of the Bogeyman all wrapped in knives and blood. His grandmother found him perched on top of the wardrobe, beyond reach and beyond tears. And, outside, the steady patter of rain on the rhododendron bushes.

'But there's no such thing as Bogeymen, David. Surely Mummy's told you that?'

'Mummy doesn't know,' said Elvis.

Johny Holy Joy had reeled on the edge of the hole, turned, slid back down the ladder so fast that next day he'd found he had no skin left on his palms though at the time of course he hadn't felt a thing, not a thing but empty as he'd run like a bleached savage with his mohawk haircut, tartan jacket, black jeans, ankles pale and blind as bean-shoots bending above his stupid big boots, bloody palms raised to shield his eyes from all the usual urban devastation dead cats dead faces dead drunks and dead ends all the way back to the post-punk squat community where he and his Mum lived now which added up to a very long run indeed.

And having found her he'd sobbed out his story, his head with its foolish plume buried in her lap. Her frightened fingers had mapped his bones and she'd thought, 'Oh God they do break, these boys, they do break so easily.' She'd advised him to keep the whole matter to himself. And he had. He hadn't been near the hospital. For one thing, there might be a policeman standing by the bed ready to grab him. For another, he didn't want to run into Rupert's mother. He was scared of the cacky old cow. She was famous for being mad and an R.C. to boot.

As time passed and nobody came round asking questions, Johny supposed, correctly, that he was free and clear of the whole barmy business.

The eyes moved: those painted eyes on the portrait of the bearded one in the beaded beanie. They looked at him.

Harold clung to the bars of his cot. He understood that protein deprivation, and whatever it was they put in the drinking water at Raleigh Manor, was affecting his mind. He understood that. There must be a way out. He'd preserve his strength. He'd bide his time. An opportunity would arise. Perhaps the next working party would provide it.

He fingered the small round wounds on his chest: her high heels. Harold bit his lip. The lovely Lady Eleanor — just his luck to have finally found his dream-woman in a dump like this. Maybe, for her sake, he'd stick around for a while.

Oh, but Jesus Christ where *was* this? Fuck! Who *were* these people?

But in his heart he knew.

There was no exit.

This was Harold's home and he had found his people.

Moss and Hazel went to Spain in a borrowed van. They went first to Burgos and then (in this order) to Valladolid, Avila, Madrid, Toledo, Cuenca, Cordoba and Seville.

'Elvis would love this,' said Moss, sitting in a sun-dappled square in this last place, sipping cold beer, holding Hazel's hand under a bashed tin table.

'No, he wouldn't,' said Hazel.

For Hazel it all came down to this: a cool stone room on a cricket-shrill hillside, the warm June night closed around them like a net, when the only words possible were probably 'I love you' though Hazel hadn't said them, and then the cut, quick, to the blythe lilting calling of her son's name as Moss flew to the telephone, which screamed the second they walked in the door, leaving Hazel to trip over her emotions and the luggage in the hall.

Walter knelt by the bed whispering his own son's name. Whenever he was alone in the room he did so. The rowdy techniques of the others upset him; the cruelly placed ice-cubes, loud music, bright lights. He yearned for gentleness to restore his violent fallen boy.

He went to the wide window high above the Common. As it was so early, shreds of the mist were still snared in the treetops.

The doctors said that a small blood vessel might have ruptured on impact and the subsequent leaking of fluid in the hours following might have been what had done the damage, but outwardly there was no sign. There was not a scratch on him, after all that. He could well be asleep, waiting only for the right piece of magic to revive him.

But that was a fate more commonly reserved for females, surely? Walter felt helpless, knowing that, in either case, a father's kiss was not required.

'Rupert,' he chided softly. 'Oh Rupert, Rupert.'

A plane crossed the sky. At any moment, Walter thought, the plane will fall, it will fall. But it didn't. A cyclist wobbled along the path that cut across the Common, past the children's corner with its swings and roundabout, the see-saw vibrating in the wind, the park-keeper's hut with its litter-strewn bed of tattered municipal marigolds, the bowling green, the vandalised bandstand, the closed café, the two tennis courts with their sagging nets. At any moment, Walter thought, the bike will fall, it will fall. But it didn't.

He was aware that he was crying. He could feel wet on his cheeks. Fielding a tear in the corner of his mouth, he could taste its salt. He was exhausted but did not sleep. He didn't feel real.

The plate glass blocked all sound. Behind his back, within the room, just the whispy hiss of oxygen, the subdued clank of medical machinery.

Walter closed his eyes. The boy, blazing like Icarus, plummeted behind his eyelids. Although he'd never suffered one, Walter knew all about those falling dreams, where, supposedly, if the dreamer ever hit bottom the dreamer was dead. On this principle Walter must always drag his eyelids apart before the boy hit the gound. But where was the ground?

His thoughts walked on fine wires with nothing above or below. Who can Walter talk to? Who is interested in listening to him? Not Daphne. She blamed him because he'd been in charge and he'd left two-thirds of a bottle of Scotch unguarded while he went to the loo. Her grief would not allow more complicated suspicions to add to her pain. Walter understood this. He found it hard.

She had been visiting friends on the Isle of Wight when it happened. And the female component of those same bloody friends having, so Walter thought, nothing better to do, had been kind enough to see her safely home and camp in the sitting room encouraging her false hopes and fantasies and cooking her scrambled eggs with chives chopped up in them.

More had dropped in since. Her mother arrived tomorrow. That was all very well. His own mother would be very welcome in the circumstances. But his father and mother were buried under two plain crosses in Rhodesia or whatever it was called now. Not that Walter didn't know what it was called now. It's just that his parents would never stomach being buried in somewhere called Zimbabwe.

Spain had bucked Moss up a lot. Since coming home she'd thought seriously about finding a well-paid job, something she hadn't thought of since before Harold and all that. With money, life would be more pleasant. That, perhaps, was the point of it. She could, for example, have a skylight installed in this room, the bedroom, to shed a bit of light. Moss smiled, her half-closed eyes lambent with pleasure as she lay on her bed imagining how it might be. Stars and rain can be seen through glass ceilings. She began to prepare a portfolio.

Moss nagged Hazel into carting those depressing albino dolls in the bedroom down to the cellar. She told Hazel she should do something sensible about it, make some less cryptic form of contact.

Hazel thought, as she stacked the dolls one on top of the other against the back of the cellar, that she too might get a job. She didn't know what she could do though. Her personality got her into trouble. How did people manage? Hazel was forty years old and didn't have a clue.

She sat in the half-dark on the cellar stairs. One of those brutes was down here. She could hear it tip-toeing about. Alexandra brushed by, squeezed around the door at the top which closed behind her. Click. It took Hazel ages to find the doorknob and when she did it came off in her hand. So now Hazel had to sit in the creepy cobwebby blackness until Moss came home to save her.

At three in the afternoon Beulah had come knocking on the front door. She'd wanted a word with Moss about something. Had Beulah known that Hazel was stuck in the cellar she wouldn't have been a bit surprised. The woods and cellars of this world are full of women like Hazel. Beulah did her bit, but she knew the bottom line. Goddess helps those who help themselves.

Sometimes, in the beginning, in the night when he'd sat there never quite believing it, and Daphne had sat opposite dozing and snuffling and making things up, and he'd not been able to break through to her by question, threat or promise nor love either, and his mind had had to run for cover, then he'd thought of Hazel.

And once, when they'd been asked to wait outside while a nurse vacuumed Rupert's lungs and Daphne had stood closed-faced in the quiet rubbery corridor, a cigarette unlit between her fingers, her smile no smile at all but just another hook to hurt him, then just that once he'd crossed the Common but there'd been nobody home. Just as well. Whatever would he have said to her after banging rudely on the door at that hour? Grief was turning him into a fifty-year-old lout.

'It's amazingly simple. Things fall apart. There's nothing you can do. Let a smile be your umbrella.'

Sod Hooper, thought Daphne. What's he on about? When she asked him to say it again Hooper feigned innocence. Entropy? No, he hadn't mentioned entropy. It was contrary to his whole philosophy, as surely Daphne should realise. Didn't she? he pressed. He wiped the baby oil from his hands with a small white towel tucked into his belt and glared at her.

Well, perhaps she did realise. She had dozed off after all. She could well have dreamt it. The words could have been her own. None the less Daphne could hardly stand the sight of Hooper these days. He'd have to go. It wasn't working. Defeat had entered into it. Not Hooper's fault, but it was there: a dark fog gathered in every corner of the room.

Flesh had dropped from Rupert. His body had stiffened into a foetal curve.

Daphne turned from the offended Hooper to stroke Rupert's face. He made a snarling noise. Anxiety picked, plucked, pricked her skin. As though a goose walked on her grave was what they said, and she could believe it too, even closed her eyes a second to see this future grave of hers lonely in driving rain, knee-keep in rotting leaves, shrouded by some dripping elm, cringing under this goose's dumb foot.

Rupert's lips were curling back from his teeth. Bubbles trapped in yellow fluid gurgled up and down in the clear tube that snaked from his nose.

'Stop it,' yelled Hooper. 'Stop messing about. You can stop it if you want.'

Daphne stared at him. She felt the twin of Rupert's horrid grin threaten her own mouth and lit a cigarette to hinder its progress.

'You shouldn't,' sighed Hooper.

"I know I bloody shouldn't. I want you to leave.'

'You don't mean that.'

'Oh but I do. I do mean that.'

Daphne had first met Hooper in the lift. Hooper specialised in dragging the unconscious back by methods many called a waste of time and some called harsh. Hooper had offered his services. But the lights, the yelling, the Souza marches, the pricking with pins, the stroking with ice, the ceaseless whispered cajoling that he sit up and take notice and put a stop to this misery once and for all — none of it had worked.

Now Hooper turned pink. He crossed to Rupert and took hold of his chin. He turned the boy's shaved head gently from side to side.

'Chin up,' he said, and choked. 'You poor little wanker,' he said and laughed, because if he didn't he'd cry. Failure.

He left the room, closing the door quietly behind him.

'I don't suppose you've heard of Pathé News?' gasped Harold.

'Of course I have, Harold,' said the Lady Eleanor. 'I was weaned on that sort of thing.'

'So many people don't understand. So many people are so young.'

'But I am not, Harold, and I do, and don't you forget it.'

Le Professeur de Judo, his face still red from the sauna, turned off the Upper Levels Highway above West Vancouver and into the Safeway parking lot. He drove slowly round until he found a space, parked his red Toyota Tercel but found that his fingers would not let go the steering wheel.

He sat there facing the glass front of the supermarket, reading the posters advising customers of that week's sale items, telling himself off.

He'd promised Lucienne he'd pick up ice-cream on his way home from the Aquatic Centre. She preferred Baskin Robbins, but because they were out of toilet tissue, orange juice and flashlight batteries and needed a new ice-cream scoop too, since their old one had gone missing some months back, he'd come here instead.

He was tired. Tote that barge, lift that bale wasn't in it as he dragged his load of bitterness down all his days.

He was scared. He couldn't face the glimpsed intimacies that lay within. Lovers shopping after work. Laying tender plans for dinner. Debating dessert.

Le Professeur had loved making dinner for Hazel while she perched on her wooden stool (they'd found it in an antique shop on a trip down the Oregon coast) lapping up her martini (he made a mean martini) and watching (but never in silence) the network news (NBC) on the small TV on top of the fridge. Hazel never missed the news if she could help it. Sometimes she fixed the salad.

Le Professeur looked at his Swatch: a gift from a student. His students didn't all give him presents, but they did all seem to like him, though why he couldn't imagine.

Almost seven. Lucienne would have been alone in the apartment for three hours now. She would have finished her homework and called her friends and now she would be starting to worry.

Men and women hurried by on each side of the car. He should move. If he couldn't handle Safeway he should at least drive on down to Baskin Robbins. He shouldn't leave her alone so much. Perhaps he should give up his swim and sauna after work, but he felt that those thirty lengths of the pool helped him keep his depression in bounds.

A tall girl with long black hair squeezed by with her sack of groceries. She knocked his sideview mirror. Le Professeur opened his door. He got out and ran the few steps needed. He took her arm and turned her to face him. She turned readily with a smile, supposing it to be someone she knew.

'You cunt,' he said. 'You fucking douche bag.'

He began to shake her. The sack tore. A stick of celery fell under their feet — cheddar cheese, a can of chilli, seaweed munchies, the new TV Guide.

'I'll kill you,' he told her.

But he didn't. Instead her lover Harriet came up behind him and took him out with a rabbit chop to the base of his neck.

As he went down, what he saw was Little Lucienne sitting alone in front of the television waiting for him to come home. He'd never felt so ashamed in his life. And when he did at last walk in with his scuffed face and no ice-cream Lucienne was very upset.

Hugging her tight, he invented a fall on the pool's slippery rim, promised her a movie downtown Friday night and dinner after in Chinatown.

He'd tried hard to make what was left of the evening pleasant, but he'd not been entirely successful. When she was in bed he'd sat staring at the closing moments of Monday Night Football, and as the Cleveland Browns stuck it to the Pittsburgh Steelers (who were missing their injured first-string quarterback in the worst way) and as his fingers tapped the arm of his chair, a terribly simple and not at all bright idea stilled his agitation. He'd knocked her down once. He could do it again. Or perhaps he'd hit on some other means. How is not the point. The point will be that in wiping Hazel from the earth he will wipe her from his mind.

Because the bus was crowded Elvis was sitting on his Mum's lap, squeezed up against the window, watching as the red light turned to green. Moss was going to show her drawings and things to some people. She looked nice. He was going to be left at his friend Jeremy's house for the day because Hazel couldn't be relied on these days.

Elvis leaned forward and buried his face in the back of the jumper of the fat man who took up most of the seat in front of them. He sniffed the comfortable smell of wet wool. Moss pulled him back, placing her arm round his waist to restrain him. The bus lurched forward. All the fat filthy raindrops slid sideways across the glass and Elvis saw him.

He stood outside a butcher's shop, sheltered by the awning, this new spiffed-up version of the Bogeyman. He was talking to an old man. The old man held a white bull-terrier by a steel choke-chain attached to a short strap of plaited leather. The Bogeyman held a handsome German shepherd on a similar leash. The old man pulled something from his pocket and held it out. The Bogeyman leaned forward slightly, stretching out his free hand to take whatever it was the old man offered, and that was all Elvis saw before the bus finally made it through the traffic lights and bore him away down Bolingbroke Grove dizzy with love.

It's not Moss.

It's not Manny, Maureen or Sue.

It's not le Professeur de Judo.

It's not Walter.

It's not any of them.

It's me.

They're all busy with their plots. So it must be me who makes this whole thing so fragmented, pointless and irritating.

As soon as she'd heard the front door close behind them, Hazel had gone to the window to gaze upon the dribbling day and to think all of the above and more. Hazel had looked without seeing, her mind lost in the distance between that place and this, this person and that.

Once Lark had asked: 'What is it you want from me?'

And once, crying on the corner of some bleak street, suspecting that Hazel had invested her with qualities she did not possess and wanting only to be alone somewhere safe indoors, sending out for pizza, watching daytime TV: 'Why do you follow me about?'

Hazel watched an intricately scarred and ancient skinhead sitting on the low brick wall opposite blow his nose on an empty crisp packet.

Buster's dented Ford Cortina pulled up outside and Beulah got out and stood looking at the house, holding the *Guardian* over her head to keep off the rain.

Hazel stepped backward, out of sight.

Beulah knocked on the door.

Hazel's thirtieth birthday fell or had fallen in April and found her sleeping in a motel room in Alamogordo, New Mexico: sleeping despite the window-blind which jittered in the morning breeze off the desert.

Television on, no sound. A preacher preaching, alternately tapping the palm of one hand with the middle finger of the other, denoting the nails of the crucifixion or an ardent request for money.

On top of the television, several items:

A thick paperback book.

A pair of traffic-cop's mirrored shades with their attendant aura of the blow-job given in exchange for the tearing up of a parking ticket, an unnecessary transaction having only to do with her need for self-abnegation at that particular time and place: an alley behind a 7-Eleven somewhere in Texas the day before yesterday. Afterwards he'd confiscated her cocaine because he'd read in *Time* magazine that trafficking in that stuff was ruining the economies of Third World countries. He'd taken her into a toilet and made her stand beside him while he flushed it away. 'Brighten the corner where you are,' he'd told her, 'That's about all we can do, I guess.' When he'd let her go Hazel had gone into the 7-Eleven and bought the thick paperback book.

A Seiko wristwatch.

A fresh pack of Camels.

A cigarette lighter in the form of the Statue of Liberty.

A fifth of Jack Daniels, plenty left.

In the bathroom pants and bra have dried overnight and hang wrinkled on the shower-rail.

On the floor Levis, white cotton shirt, blue denim jeans jacket and a pair of Frye boots purchased to replace the sick-splashed white running shoes and, in any case, more in keeping with the scene.

A dripping faucet.

The resulting rust-coloured stain on the peach-coloured porcelain.

A fly fucking another fly mid-sunbeam.

Stains of chewing tobacco sprayed on the inside of the bathroom door.

Nothing startling.

A Best Western, perhaps.

A Holiday Inn, possibly.

Hazel jumped down the stairs two three four at a time, slipped stumbled staggered but did make it to the door and down the garden path in time to catch Beulah as she was driving off. She wrenched the car door open and clung gasping to the handle.

'I've never seen you move so fast,' said Beulah.

'You've never seen me do anything.'

'This is true.' Beulah cut the engine and took a long hard look at this red-herring that had just flopped across her path.

'Please come in,' it said.

In anticipation of crisis, Beulah put the kettle on.

Hazel, wet as a tea bag, had gone upstairs to put on something dry.

Beulah sat in the kitchen waiting for the other shoe to drop.

She was not unsympathetic.

She knew what it was to stalk the world like an angry guest, refusing all amusement. She also knew that sooner or later you had to stop it. She had. Where once was ruin, storm, despair was now all peace and Buster.

Beulah examined Moss's unhappy avocado plant. She pinched the top out of it to encourage bushier, more vigorous growth.

The rain had eased. The garden bounced back, a smudge of green against the window-glass. Beulah watched a sparrow turn somersaults on the lawn as the last big drops splashed down.

The sun came out, edgy at first, but getting there.

The lone acrobat was joined by others and flew away.

Hazel was taking her time. Beulah checked her watch. She'd give her five more minutes.

One major question had to be: Where had Ms Miserable gotten all this money from?

'It fell from the sky. It hit me from behind and knocked me sideways.'

'What is that? A riddle, or what?

'No. It's not a riddle, it's the truth. I got my money by accident.'

Weird. And didn't she know her nose was running? Couldn't she feel it?

'Why me?'

Hazel wiped her nose on the cuff of Moss's old mac she'd put on over her wet nightie.

'Because you've got balls,' she said.

'I see,' said Beulah.

She didn't yet, but she fully expected to, in the end.

'Why you?'

Beulah forebore to tell. Instead she explained what had happened. How Hazel had this money and how Hazel wanted to use it to start a business to make more money.

Hazel's idea had been to open a travel agency which would organise holidays for affluent white women who wished to swap places for a time with poor women from Third World countries and really get down to the nitty-gritty. MS ADVENTURES, she wanted to call it.

Buster thought this sounded interesting but Beulah said she'd nixed it on the grounds of not being much of a money-spinner. If Hazel wanted to make real money there was only one way to do it, which was to hand over the money she already had to Avonia.

Avonia!

Buster paled. She knew all about this Avonia. Avonia wasn't just incorrect, she was heavy in the worst way. Buster didn't like it. Nor did she like Beulah going off and doing exciting things without her, leaving her to keep house. And what did she have to show for it?

'You've got the baby, babe.'

Buster walked out, slamming the door.

The baby began to cry. Beulah picked it up. Soft thoughts and old Beatles songs bubbled up in her mind. She knew she'd found her *raison d'être*.

And if she ever wished she'd found it in Boston not Balham — well, if she did, she was wise enough to keep it to herself.

Aged thirty Hazel woke up in that motel room just outside (actually)

Alamogordo and, finding she had no urgent need to pee, decided to stay in bed a while to think things over. First, though, she must secure the rattling blind. Kneeling on the bed, she saw a tall Mexican in striped pyjama pants standing on a square of dead grass watering the concrete by the pool.

Only two vehicles remained in the parking lot: the Alfa, parked skewiff across two spaces; a Winebego Super Chief with the words HOGGS MIRACLE REVIVAL CRUSADES painted in red letters along its side, parked next to a white plaster brontosaurus with blue lights for eyes. Inside the Winebego a woman sat watching *The Flintstones*. Hazel thought she should take the Alfa through a car wash today and have the finishers pay particular attention to the gas stains round the gas cap.

A Chicano maid wheeled a cart piled with fresh linen and cleaning things along the first-floor balcony of the facing units. She skirted the ice-machine, the bottles of cleaning fluids rattling together as she did so, and reached the end unit above the pool. She left the trolley, stepped to the rail and stood a moment looking down on the Mexican. He did not look up from his task. The hose trembled in his hand, sending a shivering arc of water to dimple the pool's tight surface. The maid took a key from the pocket of her overall, unlocked the door of the end unit. Hazel could see her square back in the doorway, the dark snakes of hair caught in the collar of the blue denim workshirt she wore beneath her overalls. Having checked the room, the maid stepped out of it, crossed to the balcony rail and summoned the man to her with the barest movement of her head, uttering a close-to-imperceptible moan which Hazel picked up nonetheless as all the fine hairs on the back of her neck rose in jealous antennae.

The Mexican dropped his hose, which twitched across the concrete, writhed across the face of the Coke machine and flopped over backwards into the pool. By this time he had reached the woman and, just before pushing her ahead of him into the room and shutting the door behind them with his thin brown foot, he raised the escaping coils of her hair, lifted them clear of her collar and kissed the nape of her neck in a gesture which bore the promise of such pleasure it caused Hazel to fall back on her bed as though shot.

'Don't,' instructed Hazel, 'please, please don't.' But she did. Water fell from her eyes, made lakes of her ears and dribbled out again, soaking the pillow. How long could this go on, this wanting what you can't have? How deep is the ocean? How high is the sky?

As the old geezer outside the butcher's had suggested, the Bogeyman had lined the bottom of the oven with foil to catch the blood-spatters, but what he hadn't counted on was the stink. They'd all be moaning if he didn't look out — especially that girl in the room on the top floor at the back who left snide typed notes sticky-taped up all over the place *re* cleaning the bath and the cooker after use.

The Bogeyman wondered what her problem was. She must have one or she wouldn't be here.

He slid the window up and placed a jar of Nescafé under it, so it would stay that way, and opened the oven. He took out the tray of baked liver bits the old man had given him the recipe for. They looked nice and crunchy and worked out much cheaper than dog biscuits, which was good because the Bogeyman had to watch his pennies.

He put the tray to cool on the table under the window.

Now the rain had stopped, he might take Max over to the Common for a run.

Hazel walked slowly across the Common thinking of other summers. Summers when the sun shone and the empty afternoons yawned like ovens. Was that Walter mooching along on the other side of the pond with his shoulders tucked up underneath his ears?

'Hey,' she called. 'Wait.'

Walter raised one wounded wing in salute and waited.

Buster, anxious about her anxiety, depressed about her depression, sat drinking tea out of a plastic cup at a table outside the café near the bandstand. The council had just done up the bandstand. It looked very nice, though Buster wouldn't have minded betting it would soon be wrecked again. Christ! There was Hazel with that hairy-armed Rotarian or whatever he was. See? She'd known she'd been right. Hazel was up to no good. What were these people about? People hadn't been like this in Goondiwindi. And if they had, her Dad, a recognised expert in the propagation of cactus and succulents, wouldn't have given them house room, and nor would her Mum who was famous for crocheting covers to put on empty treacle tins, turning them into footstools. Buster missed her Dad, but that wasn't the simple sort of thing you could say to anyone round here.

A pretty young man walked by with a dog of a type Buster had often seen on television busily biting one lot of people on the instruction of another lot of people, the latter usually wearing uniforms. Buster took against this dog immediately.

Angst stared at Buster and Buster stared right back as the Bogeyman stepped lightly by on feet shod in pointed shoes with silver buckles like Hamlet or something. His curly red hair bounced on his shoulders and his parchment-pale face had a nose stuck on it that could only be described as aquiline and white as the lace that frothed at his collar and cuffs.

For some reason a tear rolled down Buster's cheek and plopped into her tea.

Buster wondered if she should take the baby and go back home. This was no environment in which to raise kiddies. But then Buster thought of her Mum and those footstools and she understood, as had many another before her, that there was no going back.

At six o'clock Moss and Elvis got off the bus two stops earlier than usual so they could go to the fish-and-chip shop.

Elvis stretched up, gripped the edge of the counter and gave their order of two lots of skate and chips for Moss and Hazel and one cod and two lots of chips for himself. They'd have to wait a while for the skate.

Moss took the silver hip-flask with her deceased father's initials on it out of her handbag and had a nip of brandy. She held the flask out to Elvis who sniffed it, pulled a face, clutched his throat, fell to the floor and writhed as though poisoned.

Moss thought her interview had gone well.

What would she do if she got the job? As she screwed the top back on the flask the thought entered her mind that, in the reshuffling her life would need in order to take it, she would lose Hazel. She took the top back off the flask and took another swig.

'Drunk,' muttered Elvis from the floor.

Moss told herself she was being silly, but she knew she wasn't, even if, on the surface, it didn't make much sense.

She asked Elvis to please get up, the whole shop was watching.

She'd heard Buster and Beulah, discouraged by the demise of the Greater London Council, were talking of going to Berlin where interesting things still happened.

Moss felt dull.

Elvis beat the floor with his fists, pretending to cry.

Moss knew what he meant.

Sometimes she yearned for the pleasure of snivelling, yelping, growling and blubbering.

The pleasure of simply packing up and leaving.

But, quite honestly, where did it get you?

'Half a league, half a league, half a league onward,' roared young Albert flawlessly.

Tennyson had stopped his stutter, boosted his confidence. Miss Binns had predicted this. She'd take Tennyson over the Tavistock Clinic any day. Kipling too. There were lots of things Kipling was good for.

Every Monday, Wednesday and Friday evening Miss Binns brought Albert here, to the top of Parliament Hill, so he could fill his lungs with air and stand bellowing in the long summer dusk until street lights came on below them and it was time to stop. They'd talk quietly for a bit while Albert calmed down. Then she'd drive him home. It seemed to be working.

Dusk and the violet shadow of the helicopter fell across the land.

Rooks scattered above the silver birches. The black-and-white cows in the farthest field were gathered at their gate for milking. The Lady Eleanor stalked across the croquet lawn, headed for the helipad. Harold worked in his section of the trench, prising up rocks with a pick. Soon all the sections would be complete and the circle would be closed. Then, when the concrete was poured, the steel uprights erected and the impenetrable wire-mesh placed between them, Harold would have the satisfaction of knowing he'd played his part in putting them all behind the longest fence in the country. The Lady Eleanor had told him that it was to be even longer than that around Greenham Common, which must mean a circumference of nine miles plus, Harold thought.

Although he refused to stop and give it his full attention, Harold was aware of a scene going on in the background. This girl, who didn't pull her weight, such as it was, was screaming and weeping, her arms wrapped around a tree. She reminded Harold of that skinny witch his wife had taken up with.

Harold looked up to watch the helicopter hover above Raleigh Manor, disturbing the spiders living in the Virginia creeper which spread in a vivid rash across the face of the building.

The skinny witch was prised off the tree and carted away just in time.

The Leader had landed.

He stepped through the small square doorway and stood a moment on the top step; Father Christmas without the trimmings, fat, happy and with no death in him, so far as Harold could tell. Harold's knees shook as the light of love from those surely unearthly eyes beamed out at him, illuminating all the dark and lonely corners where ghosts and funny voices lurk.

'But wait a minute, Harold,' said his mother, driven out of one such corner and forced to take a stand.

Harold stared at the rocks that lay at his feet. He considered banging his whispy head (his hair was falling out) against the biggest one so his mother could exit through whatever orifice suited her. But mothers are not so easily dislodged.

The Lady Eleanor swept past on the arm of her master. She had no eyes for Harold despite her interest in old newsreels and the events of the night she'd walked all over him and cheered him up. She'd been bored, that was all, looking for diversion while the Leader donned his snarled tweeds and issued forth to soothe the locals' feathers which had been ruffled by the fence.

'Find a nice girl, Harold. Settle down.'

'I had a nice girl, Mum. I settled down. But it didn't work.'

'It didn't work because you ran away to India and dropped them in it.'

'I hear you,' muttered Harold, aware that he was grinding his teeth. 'It wasn't my fault.'

'Whose fault was it then, if it wasn't yours?'

'Why does it have to be like that? Why can't some things just happen and that's that? Does everything have to be somebody's fault?'

'Is the Pope a Catholic, Harold?'

At which point Harold screamed for two reasons: (1) to shut out the voice; (2) he'd stuck the pick through his foot.

But (1) didn't work because here's another voice and the worst one yet. Was it the Pope? No. Worse.

'Go ahead, Harold,' said Princess Anne. 'Block your feelings, deny your pain. Say it doesn't hurt.'

'But it does,' gasped Harold as the others ran towards him. 'My foot. It hurts. It does.'

'Not your foot fool, not your foot,' cried the impatient Princess, 'but the pain your parents taught you.'

'My father,' protests Harold. 'Only Daddy taught me pain. My mother was an innocent party.'

Harold opened his eyes. He must have fainted. He was on his back on the ground while this Princess yowled above him, her hair caught in the clouds.

'It's you, Harold. You who are the innocent party. Mummies and Daddies have secrets. They keep them in their beds at night. And Hitler,' sighed the Princess, bending nearer, 'you know about Hitler, don't you Harold?'

'I've heard,' stammered Harold from a faint and far off place in his head as he was seized beneath the armpits and jerked upright, his blood splashing down on cold stones.

'Hitler killed the innocent, Harold. It was a result of his training.'

Some distant scream drew closer and ballooned in Harold's head; seeped softly through his lips.

58

'Cry baby,' said the Lady Eleanor.

'Hum to yourself if you're sad,' said his mother.

'As a child, Harold, little Adolf was whipped, tortured and treated like a dog, if you'll excuse the figure of speech. Neither I nor any member of my family would ever wittingly be cruel to any dumb creature, with the possible exception of pheasants, peasants, fish and foxes. After many years he took revenge. As an adult he once said, "It gives us a very special, secret pleasure to see how unaware people are of what is really happening to them". '

'Sounds more like Ivy Compton-Burnett to me,' said the Lady Eleanor.

'All people are innocent,' said Harold, latching onto a word occurring a few lines back in order to stop all the others that threatened to follow, 'until we make them otherwise.'

'Who's this we, white man?' screeched the Princess flapping skywards and dragging all the weather with her.

The stars had been fleeting, glimpsed through moving clouds as they'd lain together on their bed of leaves in the bushes near the boating lake in Battersea Park.

'This is silly,' Walter had said. 'Next time we must go to a hotel.'

Hazel sank beneath him, curled up laughing in the leaves. She stroked his face. He caught her hand and held it to his lips.

'Tell me,' she'd said.

Walter had said nothing. He'd had no intention of broadcasting his own bleak needs. He felt lonely: stuck between those landmarks his American grandmother had always referred to as being the rock and the hard place.

'I'd better go home,' he'd said.

Moss had eaten her own fish and chips ages ago and, at ten o'clock, she'd heated up Hazel's and eaten them as well. What she'd most like now was a cup of tea, but she couldn't be bothered moving. She liked sitting here on the stairs with the front door open to the quiet street with whatever chill there was in the night kept at bay by her mother's shawl resting lightly across her shoulders. Laughter blared from the Fishers' TV and abruptly died.

She thought about Harold. Let him be all right.
She thought about Hazel. Ditto.

Buster still wasn't back.

Why couldn't Beulah have kept her big mouth shut and why couldn't everything still be like it had been in the beginning? Like that first Christmas when everyone Beulah knew had been out of town and Buster had turned up on the doorstep of her flat in Ladbroke Grove bearing gifts and wearing her WOMEN AND TURKEYS AGAINST CHRISTMAS badge.

Buster had bought a goose, two bottles of wine and a plum pudding from Harrods. She'd also brought *The Fontana Biographical Companion to Modern Thought* as a Christmas present for Beulah. Beulah had given Buster her only copy of Tee Corinne's *Cunt Coloring Book*.

They'd lain together to look at it on the mattress on the floor in front of the single-bar radiator and then they'd made it together for the first time.

Afterwards Buster had cried because she'd liked it so much and it had been so long since she'd done it and because they'd been guilty of practising a style of love-making often put down by the politically correct as being imitative of heterosexual intercourse and because she'd indulged in gender swapping fantasies.

Beulah had been so intrigued by all this unexpected innocence and drama that had landed in her lap that she'd failed to notice how the combination of greasy goose and filthy oven had caused first the stove and then the kitchen curtains to catch fire.

The drunk who lived in the basement had phoned everyone she could think of, and in the end the fire-brigade, but by then it was too late and the house had burned down.

After so promising a beginning Beulah felt she had to ask herself how come it was that now the whole thing was falling to ratshit.

Three big hunchbacks crowded through the doorway, causing Moss's heart to beat faster until they showed themselves to be

Manny, Maureen and Sue wearing backpacks and wanting to know if they could spend the night in her front room. The space they usually occupied in a Bermondsey warehouse was filled by others because the three had returned one day early from their annual holiday in Lyme Regis, though why this was so they did not say.

Moss said yes.

Manny, Maureen and Sue dropped their packs and surged down the hall and into the kitchen to make themselves bacon and eggs and fried bread. As they ate they told Moss all about their holiday.

For four years now they'd gone to stay for a fortnight in an eighteenth (Sue said) century house run by women for women on a bed and breakfast basis.

They always took the same room, which was at the back of the house, overlooking the sea and the whole Golden Cap area.

Moss wondered about this Golden Cap. She pictured pixies and elves and thought how exhausted she was. She watched Manny eating and decided you could tell a lot about a person by the way they tackled an egg.

In this room with its view of whatever it was, Manny, Maureen and Sue had eaten peaches and almonds and made love all day except when they'd left it to walk five miles along the coast to Axminster, a famous town where Mary Anning, a lost woman of herstory, who'd been born in 1799, first discovered fossils on the Lyme and Charmouth beaches.

Happily Moss remembered the approximate inch of Canadian Club that remained in the bottle on the shelf beside the cookery books.

'I'm glad you enjoyed yourselves,' she said, getting up to fetch it. Maureen looked up from her plate and smiled.

'And you. What have you been up to?'

'This and that,' said Moss, pouring the rye into a glass. She put the bottle gently down on the draining-board and turned to face the three women seated around her table. If they hadn't been there she would have had to phone her mother because her need to say what she was going to say was urgent.

'I'm taking a job. In an advertising agency. It will mean I won't be able to work with the Collective any more. I'm sorry.' Which was a bit rich, considering she hadn't even got the job yet.

Manny looked at Maureen. Maureen looked at Sue. Then they all looked at Moss.

'You see,' said Manny, 'things do work out.'

Sue took the glass from Moss. She put her arm round her and proposed a toast.

'To the end of the Collective.'

'Oh, I wouldn't say that,' murmured Moss modestly.

'What? What wouldn't you say?' asked Hazel as she walked in. A large dead leaf clung to the front of her cardigan and she was in no mood for mysteries.

'We're disbanding our Collective,' said Manny, 'because we're going to open a garage and she's going into advertising.'

'People still do that, do they?' asked Hazel, going to the stove and turning on the gas. She struck a match, plucked the large dead leaf from the front of her cardigan and dropped it onto the flame. It rose blazing toward the ceiling. Sue flapped at it with a tea-towel.

'Look out,' Manny said.

'Outside Lyme Regis,' said Maureen, as if Hazel could care less.

Buster came back and Beulah made her a cup of tea and gave her two librium and got into bed with her. They talked for a while, and then had sex, and after that Buster felt more mettlesome.

When Buster slept, Beulah got up. She needed to sit alone in the dark and think about Avonia. She needed to be very clear on what she wanted to say to her when she called Fort Worth at midnight. Avonia was tricky. Avonia could jump either way. Avonia had these CIA connections forged in the Fall of '71, or so the rap went, when she'd been with the Marine Supply Corps at Da Nang.

'Travellin' do broaden one's scope, girl,' was all Avonia had ever had to say about it, sometimes adding, 'I owes a lot to the military and I don't care who knows it.' Eleven forty-five.

Beulah closed her heavy-lidded eyes and pictured herself back on the bottom with Avonia on top demanding to know if she didn't just love being fist-fucked by the ideological enemy. 'Like slowly putting on a hot, tight, wet satin glove,' she'd whispered unexpectedly because that definitely hadn't been in the script, though the rest of it pretty much had as she'd placed her knee in the small of Beulah's back and run a finger down her spine. 'Relax, honey. It's cool so long as you knows what you're doin'. I been around, babe. I seen things even in the stomach of my Mammy and she's eighty-six now and still with us, I's happy to say. I done this to lots of chicks. They's beggin' for more by the time I'm through. What we need here is a little Crisco.' This last to her brother, Avis, crouched behind the camera in his LAPD uniform.

Hard to believe now that she'd ever been into all that. She didn't regret it. She'd learned much from Avonia about the essential sadness of power.

Beulah took herself into the kitchen to make a mug of hot chocolate. She much preferred coffee of course, but these days that stuff turned her stomach straight to acid. All part of the aging process, she supposed. Where were the marshmallows? Where had Buster, ever anxious that Beulah watch her weight, hidden them this time?

Hazel walked beneath the belly of the brontosaurus toward the Copper Kettle Coffee Shop. The Winebego had gone. Hazel dropped a quarter into a blue metal box and slid out a copy of the *Alamogordo American Statesman*. She went into the coffee shop, took a back booth and ordered a plain waffle and coffee. Four cops talked Black Holes at the counter behind her. Hazel read her paper and ate up her waffle. She decided to drive to the coast where she knew someone in Huntington Beach who'd buy the Alfa for cash. Then she'd head north for Canada, which is where le Professeur de Judo is waiting to come into it one wet night on a cross walk in the following November. On her way out Hazel stopped at the motel lobby to buy a postcard of the brontosaurus. In this picture its eyes have come out green. She still has it, somewhere.

A silver scimitar sliver of a moon was pinned high beyond the window. Beulah kept her eye on it as she stuck her felt-tip in the hole and dialled the first digit. She hesitated, broke the connection, started again. Click click click and Beulah was down there with the fishes, seeing the transatlantic cable burrowing wormlike and purposeful over the ocean floor, skirting the *Titanic*, the dead U-boats and all that, even though she knew that these days the whole thing was done up in the sky, slightly to the left of that pretty brooch of a moon.

One ring in Fort Worth and the phone was snatched up.

'Este numero no es . . . no es . . .' came a male voice.

'No es what?' prompted Beulah.

'Safe,' snapped the voice and hung up.

Beulah picked up her hot chocolate and drew comfort from the steam that rose round her nose. Beulah felt funny. Felt the world shift a bit, become a cold place suddenly; or perhaps not so suddenly. It seemed an unhappy thing to lose touch with someone you'd been close to. Avonia flared before her in the darkness, trapped forever in the brightly lit sideshow of angry sex.

'Avonia?' whispered Beulah, wondering if she were having a paranormal experience and how she'd cope if she was. Would she tell anyone, for example? How could you explain a thing like that without sounding like an idiot? No matter. It was just Buster standing in the doorway framed in curdled yellow light from the bare bulb in the hall. Buster looked from Beulah's startled face to the telephone receiver in her hand.

'What are you doing?'

The enormity of any such explanation overwhelmed Beulah. The contrast between the mad and glorious Avonia born in flames of blazing rage, and doubtless dying in similar fashion, and Buster Brown from Goondiwindi looking daggy in the army surplus gear left over from those brief days of daring when she'd belonged to Militant Tendency and had just dragged on over her pyjamas in an effort to keep warm was more than Beulah could usefully contemplate. She uncoiled from her armchair, sprang across the length of worn carpet that separated them and thumped Buster's head against the doorframe.

Once she was safely back in her armchair Beulah felt a bit ashamed and slightly sleepy. She had acted badly. But, she told herself sensibly, such displays, though enthralling at the time, are irrelevant in what is usually referred to as the long run. Beulah felt that, as an aging primate sitting alone in the dark, she had a pretty good grip on the finer points of the long run. She could also recognise a low point when she saw it. The thing was now to go to sleep and expect that things would be better in the morning. She found her old sleeping-bag and the thin bit of foam that went under it in the sideboard. It smelt musty, but never mind. She couldn't face getting back into bed beside the doubtless still snivelling Buster. She put the sleeping-bag down in front of the dying coal fire, got into it and lay there for a while. Then she got up again and crossed the hall to the baby's room. She picked it up and carried it back to the sleeping-bag. She knew she shouldn't do this because, according to Buster, she might roll on the baby and squash it in her sleep. She decided to risk it. She squeezed the baby tight. She understood her hold on it was tenuous. She had no claim on it. All she'd done was hand over an old Beatles album to the milkman, the one with them dressed up as butchers on the cover, cutting up dolls. The milkman had been after it for years and a yoghurt carton full of semen was a small price to pay. The thing was worth a small fortune these days. They'd never believe him down, or was it up, at the pub. Beulah covered the priceless baby with kisses. It screwed up its face against them and managed to stay asleep. Beulah slept too. In the morning the baby woke unsquashed and jolly as ever. The same could not be said for Buster and Beulah.

Moss's Mum was waltzing round her kitchen to the music of Guy Lombardo with this nice widower from two doors down with whom she had sexual intercourse twice a week, when her daughter rang to tell her that she'd landed this job designing adverts in magazines and the like.

Clarice was so delighted that those years at Art School had meant something after all that she opened a bottle of bubbly there and then, though it was barely ten in the morning. She and the widower clinked glasses.

'To the ladies, God love 'em,' he said.

A febrile excitement fuels le Professeur de Judo's own constant and jittery dance, sends him waltzing into a travel agent on Robson Street to pick up an airline ticket, spins him into the health food store on the next block to pick up some Trail Mix to snack on as he cycles to work.

Walter didn't know what to say to Daphne. He had no desire to go to work. What was happening? Why couldn't they be kinder to each other? All he could think of was Hazel. He must see her today. This afternoon. But what for?

This morning he'd sit with Rupert.

'He's got someone,' said Daphne to herself when he'd put his hat on and gone, 'some physically perfect eighteen-year-old innocent he's screwing senseless,' and she lit a cigarette and sipped coffee grown cold, black and bitter as her heart.

Harold lies coiled on the Aubusson carpet in the downstairs drawing-room looking up Moon Baby III's skirt and, finding no particular comfort there, he begins to cry.

Distant music, rhythmic groaning, the Nuremburg Rally, or it may just be his fever that he hears.

Leaf shadows from the *Salix matsudana 'Tortuosa'* growing outside the window flicker across the elegantly proportioned prospect of white, of gold, of green brocade; crown briefly the tender charcoal head of one of Sargent's boys, likewise the Romney children on the far wall before moving on to enliven the protruberant eyes of a young woman Moon Baby III cannot help but think was let down rather badly by Gainsborough. She also thinks that Harold must lose his foot, and she should know because in real life Moon Baby III was a doctor. Of course that Gainsborough may simply be hung in a spot that fails to do it justice. Looking more closely Moon Baby III begins to think this likely. Stepping over Harold she moves toward an empty place on the end wall of the drawing-room between two cabinets that she thinks would serve it better.

The Lady Eleanor enters.

'Fascist,' sighs Harold happily.

'Please don't exaggerate,' snaps the Lady Eleanor. 'Exaggeration and generalisation are the two great abiding sins of your particular generation.' The Lady Eleanor turns to Moon Baby III to back her on this one, but Moon Baby III, unwilling to be caught up in other people's mind games, has levitated and sits beneath the finely-turned vault of the ceiling. 'Blimp,' rails the Lady Eleanor.

Moon Baby III makes no reply, looks down on them small-faced and reconsiders this matter of the Gainsborough. The truth is that the Leader has hung it there simply to cover the pale patch left by the Rembrandt when he'd taken it away to the bunker beneath the Mojave where, it was to be hoped, both he and it would survive Armageddon, scheduled for April next year. The English pictures, on their small scale (though masterly, of course), he was content to leave where they were, finding them soothing to come home to.

When the Lady Eleanor departs, Moon Baby III floats gently down.

'Don't push the river, Harold,' she advises, 'it flows.'

They'd looked through the *Guinness Guide to Feminine Achievements* and decided to name their garage after Gwenda Stewart, who'd been a racing driver in the 1920s. She'd been into motorbike racing too, and had driven ambulances during the war and rafted down the Yukon River and broken car speed records.

It was expected that GWENDA'S GARAGE would cater mostly for women customers, which wasn't to say that men wouldn't be welcome — they would, provided they didn't try to take the piss out of women mechanics in any way whatsoever.

Manny, Maureen and Sue left next morning to start their new life while Hazel was still asleep, though Moss and Elvis got up to wave them off.

Maureen pulled a fleecy sweatshirt out of her pack and gave it to Elvis because it had shrunk. When they'd gone he spread it out on the kitchen table and looked at it. He liked the bright yellow colour, but when he turned it over it had the words GIVE A GIRL A

SPANNER printed in bold black across the back.

'If I did,' he said, 'if I did give a girl a spanner, what would she do with it?'

'The same things that you would,' replied Moss.

Elvis picked up an imaginary spanner and brought it down on top of his head.

'Bop,' he said, 'Tweet, tweet, tweet.'

And 'Ouch!' says the Bogeyman.

He has cut his finger opening a tin of Soppy Pup, or whatever it's called.

He goes outside and searches in vain through the dustbins for a re-usable bandaid.

He goes upstairs to see if the girl in the room on the top floor at the back can help him. He knows she is there because, after all, she never goes out.

She opens her door.

Her name is Renate.

Love at first sight, thinks the Bogeyman. That's what it must be, this reeling feeling.

'Come in,' says Renate, hoping he has come to discuss the state of the bathroom. She closes the door.

Angst, who has followed his master up the stairs, inserts his nose in the space under the door and sighs.

This being a Monday, Iris Tatters had let herself in at 8.30 to clean. She hadn't yet looked in to say hello to Daphne because she'd run out of suitable things to say to a woman whose eldest son is in a coma, and anyway Daphne's incomprehensible jokes made her nervous.

Daphne heard the dull thud thud which was Iris sweeping the back stairs. The stairs the children use most; all the window ledges piled with toys, books, broken and forgotten things. The dark back stairs where, on narrow January days, it was Daphne's habit to stand at one or other of the windows on one or other of the landings to watch the engorged red suns of winter hang low in the sky: so low, it would seem to Daphne, as to be in danger of impaling themselves on the spikes of the black iron railings on the edge of the Common, and then what a tide of red would rise to drown them all beneath cold skies smeared with those screaming parrot colours caused by trans-national pollutants identified by number not by name, or not by any name that Daphne knew.

Moss whirled out to the dustbins with some exhausted tea leaves wrapped in newspaper, and who should she find there but Buster with a bloody bit of bandage patched to her forehead, because Beulah, it seemed, had suddenly turned into a wife-beater. Also, she was trying to use Hazel's money to set up some sort of dodgy business with the CIA.

Buster was keen to know what Moss thought.

Moss thought this was nonsense in light of the fact that Hazel rarely had enough money to pay so much as her own bus fare, but naturally she did not say so, Hazel's financial situation being no concern of Buster's, nor of Mrs Fisher's either, and she was bound to be listening behind the hedge. Instead she invited Buster in and made her coffee though there were several things she would have preferred to be doing. Clothes, for instance. She'd like a new outfit to start off with.

'Beulah's sold out,' said Buster, the antipodean whine bleeding back into her voice as it tended to do in moments of stress. It occurred to Moss that she no longer fancied Buster. She thought of Hazel upstairs, snoring away in her BEAM ME UP, SAPPHO T-shirt, doubtless still wrapped up like a sausage in the duvet, her long feet in those silly socks with the multi-coloured toes sticking out at the end, and it came to Moss that she didn't fancy anyone much any more. The hairs on her legs didn't grow so vigorously these days either. Moss wondered if the two things were connected.

Later on Buster went home and Moss sent Elvis outside to play while she went upstairs to have things out with Hazel.

Just before Buster gets home a letter comes for Beulah. The scent of sex, jasmine and juleps fills the flat as Beulah opens it, which cheers things up a lot.

Beulah pours herself a shot of bourbon remembering kisses in a garden in Lafayette, Tennessee, but they'd had to be careful because there'd been a gossip columnist at this party and discretion was the better part of whatever it was. 'But one day, honey,' her Southern Belle had breathed and that day, it seemed, was drawing near. She'd be staying at the Savoy, but would prefer that they meet at Brown's Hotel for afternoon tea. It was signed 'in anticipation'.

'You bet your sweet ass,' said Beulah.

Daphne's dozed off on the sofa in the upstairs drawing-room. Even Iris doesn't have the heart to wake her. Instead she takes her money from the Coronation biscuit tin on the dresser in the basement kitchen and tiptoes to the Nightingale.

Daphne won't go to the hospital this afternoon. When she wakes up, she will decide to go to the High Street and shop for food. Then she will prepare dinner and make them all sit down together to eat it.

This will please Albert, Felicity, Benjamin, Felix and Dominic very much though it's doubtful that their father will be there.

Footsteps on the stairs announce that Moss advances.

Hazel sees her mother lying dead on the floor.

The image crashes down on the bare boards between Hazel and the bedroom door, between Hazel and escape.

She never knows when this image will come, but here it is and there's no way round it, really. Mum, stone dead in Goondiwindi and nobody about but Hazel.

No sound either, other than that made by fruit gently rotting in the cut-glass bowl on the sideboard.

Was there never, anywhere, ever any consolation to be found for having been born a girl?

Hazel jumps into her jeans and hurtles to the window.

'Rien,' echoes le Professeur de Judo's empty heart as he guns his car through the wastes of New Westminster and the summer seediness of White Rock, where the wrenching stench of rotting seaweed forces him to roll up the window.

Because it is Sunday he must wait in a long tail-back of cars before passing through the border checkpoint.

He's going down to Seattle to purchase a firearm, which he will bring back hidden somewhere in his car this evening.

He does not expect that any of this will be a problem. Then, quite soon, he'll be on his way to give Hazel something to cry about.

While he's doing this Little Lucienne will travel to Montreal, where she will be cared for by his Maman.

This is how the story ends: gurgling with rage, Rumpelstiltskin grabs his left foot and tears himself in two. The book containing this information is lying open on the grass where Elvis dropped it.

Inspired, Elvis has taken his own left foot and tugged and heaved and hopped all round the lawn. But it's impossible, that sort of thing, except in the relevant fairytales.

Hazel drops out of the sky behind Elvis, hits the ground running.

Elvis laughs, cheered by the fact that ladies can come from clouds.

Behind his back and above his head a rope of tied-together sheets dangles whitely over the window sill, flapping slightly in the breeze. Or is it Moss's hot cross breath that stirs them as she puts her head out the window to watch Hazel fleeing up the road?

Moss cannot understand why Hazel runs from confrontation and the subsequent possibility of comfort; the simple bliss of sorting things out. One day Moss fully expects to find Hazel with her head caved in, not by Moss of course, but surely someone would oblige, 'which would be a bit triste for her, I think,' says Sue as she comes into the bedroom unseen and unannounced, making Moss jump.

Sue has gone with the others as far as the tube before missing her hat and coming back to fetch it. But now what does this Sue person think she's doing as she leans closer to Moss and murmurs, 'Things unravel,' and then, intruding further, expands the thought to include 'string bags, affairs of the heart,' and then closes the gap by kissing Moss's mouth?

Sue thinks she is bringing comfort where comfort is due, and she is right. Lying with her on the unsheeted bed Moss feels a sparkle start up round her heart which tells her that life is worth the effort.

Later on Moss and Sue look everywhere, but neither is able to find the hat. Sue decides that she must have dropped it in the street, or possibly left it somewhere else entirely.

It's so bright outside. Hot, even. On the Common, people take their clothes off and sit in their underwear, retaining their shoes and socks.

Sharp sunlight picks on bits of broken milk-bottles in the road. Unseemly plants force their way through cracks in the pavement, making the way impassable.

The asphalt bubbles and sticks to Hazel's socks with the multi-coloured toes. She is in danger of being glued to the spot.

An old man, locked in argument with an invisible other, walks briskly by. Hazel has never been this way before. She's just passed a house with a tropical landscape painted across its front. This mural was the handywork of the psychiatric social worker who'd painted it the summer before last. He'd been assisted by those of the house's inhabitants who'd felt like it. The ironmonger round the corner had donated the paint in all the unpopular colours that people would not buy.

The outside of this house is bad enough. It's worse inside. There's all this tabloid behaviour going on.

Harold wants to go to a proper hospital, and after that he wants to go home. He seems to have forgotten that he no longer has any such thing. Unless of course he means that he wants to go into a Home, which could be arranged.

Harold blames everyone and everything but himself for his predicament. He blames his father. He blames his mother. The Lady Eleanor despises this all too common habit. Clearly he has not been listening. She had given him the Leader's healing chart as soon as his troubles had started. There it was: all he needed to know, right there in black and white between gallstones and gas-pains:

Problem	Cause	Cure
Gangrene	Mental morbidity. Drowning of joy with poisonous thoughts.	I now choose harmonious thoughts and let the joy flow through me.

But Harold had taken no notice, so now he had had to lose his foot.

The Lady Eleanor wondered what her next step should be.

She decided to lock him up in the south turret along with a wretch of a girl who refused to take responsibility for her own epilepsy.

Problem	Cause	Cure
Epilepsy	Sense of persecution Rejection of life. A feeling of great struggle. Self-violence.	I now choose to see life as eternal and joyous. I am eternal and joyous and at peace.

They could work on their charts together — see if, between them, they couldn't work up a bit of joy.

What is the Bogeyman doing to the girl called Renate in the upstairs room at the back?

Why is she pleading with him in Spanish?

Why is Angst whining and clawing at the woodwork of the door to get out, having once clawed and whined so hard to get in?

Why does Renate cry out to her absent mother in Dutch?

And where is the psychiatric social worker?

Why are these people never about when you need them?

Then comes a final cry in a language too terminal to determine.

It's nearly time for Rupert to make a decision.

He knows they're out there, the ones who want him back. He senses their presence as a fish, suspended in the safe black water beneath the thick sea-ice, senses the still presence of the Hunter.

To swim away into silence and darkness or to burst upwards into pain, noise, trouble?

The first option attracts him but something holds him where he is.

It's all right though.

There's still a bit of time.

He's not going anywhere yet.

As a matter of fact he's waiting for someone.

He doesn't know who.

But when this person comes — then he will know.

Elvis had borrowed Sue's hat to go to the lavatory in and, when he had, he'd called his mother to see the little white worms wiggling in his shit.

As they walked to the chemist to purchase the appropriate pills, Moss shuddered to think that human beings could harbour such parasites even though she knew that their bodies, hearts and minds are open-house to all sorts of parasites, all the time.

Elvis took his mother's hand.

'I dreamed you were a door and that you shut,' he told her. Moss gave the primeval little brute a good whack on the bum. The desire to do so had been building up in her all morning.

Hazel's way off track. She doesn't recognise this place at all. The hot gritty wind irritates her eyes and wraps old newspapers and torn plastic carrier bags round her legs.

Women in turquoise saris, pink knitted cardigans, socks and sandals hurry by looking neither left nor right nor anywhere at all lest someone bash them up.

At Hazel's approach the tube's mouth belches up a smell of piss and chips so strong it makes her gag. The smacked-out troglodytes who live round the corner in big cardboard boxes brush blindly by. Children, all of whom are missing something important — a nose, their hair, some fingers — gibber and beg and tumble in the dust.

Has there been an accident?

Once there was. Not here but a long way away.

Instructions were given out on the television at the time. Stay out of the rain. Don't be silly. Wash all fruit before eating.

Precautions were taken. Certain foodstuffs buried at sea.

Some connection is possible, though nothing is clear.

Renate hadn't expected death to come to her here.

Six months ago they'd all expected death to come, every night, trying to sleep a little, guarding the precious medical supplies, praying light would come soon, knowing that at any moment one of the Government's Death Squads could come screaming out of the darkness and tear off their faces.

In that place Renate had expected death. Not here. It didn't seem reasonable.

A pretty palm of dusky pink smacks flat against the dirty glass inside the ticket window. Hazel, who's in no mood to mess about, gives it the finger, jumps the turnstile and hurries to the escalators.

Down she goes past all the bright advertisements imperturbable behind the ranks of paper tigers, those scribbled thickets of thickly crayoned cocks which bob before them like dirigibles, such easy targets after all, born aloft on hairy inflated balls. Bang, thinks Hazel. Pop that prick. Prick that pope. Rat-tat-tat. Was that Freud a nut or not? 'Everybody says so, all our friends,' sings Hazel as she enters echoing corridors where thick green water drips and an ill-wind from the underground howls across the face of ill-spelt messages writ large in blood and emerges onto a platform at the end of which is Walter waiting for a train.

'Take me somewhere nice,' she says.

Ought he? Should he? He does.

The Bogeyman packs Renate neatly into the fridge. Some of her in the main part and some in the freezer compartment for later. This is by no means an easy thing. It takes him a long time. When he's done it, the Bogeyman removes his lace cuffs, rinses them under the cold tap and hangs them on the brass rail at the foot of her bed to dry.

'You are so nuts!' screamed Hazel, taking Lark by the collar of her expensive and presumably new tweed jacket outside a Chinese market on the lower West Side owned by Mr Bing Lee senior and operated by Mr Bing Lee junior, and shaking her and noticing that she'd done something to her hair too, while her back was turned. It was shades lighter and curlier. It seemed she'd got a job too, as one of the floor-managers on the Phil Donahue Show. But why?

'Because you've got to start somewhere,' Lark said. What kind of reason was that? They were taping this afternoon, as a matter of fact. They were starting at 2.30. The issue was to be transvestites in the Pentagon. Which was why Lark really had to go now.

'Don't you know what you're doing? Don't you know how long a time we're dead? Forever and ever,' sobbed Hazel who, despite her decision to the contrary, had turned right round after her waffle and driven back to New York to have this disastrous lunch at the Russian Tea Room some days later with Lark because she couldn't accept it yet about the waiting grave and death and being alone forever and ever, even before you're dead, and (this above all) about Lark not wanting to grab whatever could be grabbed from the here and now because today was all there was, is all there is. Hazel took the keys to the Alfa and put them in Lark's top pocket.

'You can have it, have my car.'

'I don't want your car.'

'But it's a terrific car,' wailed Hazel.

'Oh shit,' sighed Lark. 'Get real.'

A long silence.

Lark had this look on her face, like she was being made to eat okra. What did Hazel think she was doing, standing in the middle of the sidewalk with her eyes shut tight and refusing to let go her lapel? Was she on something, or what? What if someone Lark knew came by? Phil Donahue, for instance?

A derelict squatted in the street, greasy pant-legs rolled above scabby knees, hair hanging in filthy vines to obscure features already dimmed by dirt. He was tapping out rhythms only he could hear, using two slats from an orange crate as drumsticks against an iron manhole cover. He was just the image Lark needed, bobbing on her horizon like a lifeboat; she flung herself into it with gratitude.

'Different drummers,' she said softly.

'What? Where?'

'There.'

Hazel released Lark's collar and turned. Taxis and cars swerved round the derelict. Hazel could hardly bear to look. He was her age too; possibly younger. Lark, feeling safe and therefore able to be generous, reached out and stroked Hazel's arm.

'It wouldn't work, Hon. Try to understand. I'm sorry,' she added, which was true.

'I'm always so afraid I'll end up like that,' whispered Hazel turning back to the only person standing, or so it seemed to Hazel then, between her and such a fate, but Lark, who had her own life to save, had gone and for good this time.

Where? Where the fuck had she gone? Hazel burst into the Chinese market, raged up and down the aisles crammed with cans of shark's fin soup and jars of freeze-dried scorpions and old bits of tree in cellophane packets and lark's tongues. Lark's tongues? Oh irony. Oh misery, and who buys all this crap anyway? Hazel wanted to know, and perhaps she asked because several faces not a bit inscrutable but more on the astonished side turned towards her, and then she was out on the street again listening in disbelief at the appalling sexist patter pouring from the mouth of the Shill outside the Pussycat Theatre next door which was just opening its doors for the day. That well-known different drummer was nowhere in sight.

Mr Lee senior, who went back a long way, having come to this country seventy-nine years ago to set up market gardens in Queens or somewhere dumb like that, danced across the sidewalk on his tiny Chinese feet, an orange bright in his left hand.

'Whachuwan?' His voice tearing; frail as ricepaper. Hazel hit him. Mr Lee senior folded silently into the gutter. The orange flew from his hand. His plastic teeth flew from his head and nattered toward a storm drain. A quick kick from Hazel helped them down into the city sewer. Understanding that none of this was likely to endear her to anyone, Hazel ran away as fast as she could.

When she finally remembered where she'd parked the Alfa of course she didn't have the rotten keys, so she walked off and left it where it was, somehow entertaining the thin fantasy that Lark would find it and drive it and love her for it and somehow find the courage to quit working for Phil Donahue.

What next was the question. She thought of phoning the Samaritans, but there wasn't a phone booth in sight that hadn't been ingeniously reduced to a knee-high blob of melted plastic.

A black super-stretch pulled up at the stop-light beside her.

Hazel opened one of the back doors and fell inside. Two sheeted figures seated in a jacuzzi looked up from their rum and cokes. A snuff movie flickered on the video, giving Hazel a clue.

'I'll suck you both off if you'll take me to the airport,' cried she attempting a dive into their tents. They fought her off with hands like hooks, stitched up their flaps, and threw her out before the limo had even started to slow for the next light. In high weedy voices of indeterminate sex they informed the driver that he was fired for failing to take care of their security. As the thing drove off the driver stared back at Hazel in the sideview mirror. It looked to Hazel as though he might be crying, but other people's concerns were no concern of hers as she sat in the street with mid-town traffic whirling round her wondering if she'd reached the place they called rock bottom and whether, this being the case, she could now expect there to be nowhere to go but up.

A gorgeous child came dancing along, curly whisps of marijuana leaves poking from her hair.

'Take it to the limit,' howled a bunch of voices from this kid's blaster.

'Yeah, take it to the limit.' The kid turned the sound up. 'Just take it to the limit one more time.'

Buildings blurred and flew away. The girl span, skipped, strutted, whirled and winked at Hazel. Hazel laughed. Hazel howled. Hazel roared her approval. Hazel regained the pavement. Hazel felt better.

'New York, New York it's a wonderful town,' hummed Hazel. One way or another she always had a good time here. Except for this whole Lark thing of course — but that could've happened anywhere.

Hazel was beginning to feel a bit sorry for Lark, but if what that girl wanted was to throw her life away and end up as some kind of superwife holding down a nine-to-five job what was there to say? No one could say that Hazel hadn't done her best to turn her around.

A good man with a gun above his heart. It rests inside his tracksuit. With the passing days a faint bruise spreads. On this day smoke from the slash-burning taking place on the far side of the estuary hangs above the water and blurs the line of mountains to the north. The great geese clatter overhead; departing, always departing in a thin line round the world.

Le Professeur de Judo smacks himself down on the sand and begins his press-ups. He welcomes the thought of the coming winter. Cold can be a sedative. The cool amber waves roll in. A buoy sounds a warning in the dangerous shallow water beyond. It is a single sad and hollow note.

He should heed it.

'Get real,' Lark had said.

Well, Hazel is doing her best. She's standing in line at a Greyhound Bus Station to buy a ticket to anywhere in Canada, and you can't get realer than Canada.

A small domestic tableau springs to mind:

Int.	Lark's loft.	Night.

Lark, exhausted from her labours on the Donahue Show, is telling Steven with the bad back all about her horrid lunch with Hazel. Steven makes Lark a comforting cup of camomile or some such weakly tea while their cat, a hideous thing that Hazel had at first sight supposed to be the remains of a medical experiment but which Lark'd said was a Cornish Rex and therefore meant to look like that, sat farting on the fake Welsh Dresser.

Slow fade to black.

Hazel sniffed and looked over the shoulder of the faggot in front of her who was flicking through the latest *Cosmo* — looking for the page with the horoscopes on it. When he found it his lilac nails scratched down the page like chicken's claws in search of his sign.

Hazel stood on tiptoe to see what Taurus had to say, but he got wise to her and flipped the page before she could read it. He was taking his smashed immune system home to Saskatoon to lay it at the feet of his neanderthal father, so why should he be nice?

Someone up ahead, too stoned to stand, fell over and the line shuffled forward. The faggot bought his one-way ticket and there was Hazel face to face with destiny. She said the first thing that popped into her head, which happened to be Vancouver, and so that is where she went.

Moss went to Harrods. She took Elvis with her. They went to the pet department to buy all the things you need to start an aquarium. They could just as well have got everything down the market on Saturday morning, and a lot cheaper too, but Elvis had so much wanted to do it this way and Moss had given in because she was obscurely guilty about the fact that she was about to start going out to work and he'd be going to nursery school and that, in the end, he'd have to grow up like everybody else and realise that aquariums don't grow on trees. Besides, Moss had a soft spot for Harrods. Once, due to a financial crisis, she'd worked there during a January sale, in the Men's Knitwear Department. Taking advantage of the staff discount she'd bought Harold a pair of cashmere socks in the loveliest cerulean blue but she supposed he'd have mislaid them somewhere along the way. Where was Harold? She thought she might try and find out, in case Elvis ever asked, or her mother.

They brought all the stuff home by bus, which was hell. Elvis clung grimly through all the changes and jostling and lurching to his slopping plastic bag of fish and the blue plastic diver which he intended to put, as a finishing touch, on the coloured plastic gravel at the bottom of the tank. Moss wrestled with everything else. Kind ladies past child-bearing age would keep smiling at Elvis and patting their laps in invitation, but Elvis kept a stern grip on things and his mother and scowled into the middle distance to avoid their eyes.

Harrods would have delivered, but not straight away this minute, which was absolutely no good of course, as Moss had told them, feeling totally in sympathy with Elvis's trembling lower lip. Moss still hadn't managed to buy herself so much as a new pair of tights. Never mind. Perhaps tomorrow.

The second they got in he insisted they set about putting the aquarium together. Moss made them a cup of tea, took three aspirin and set about it. Nothing fit with anything. The instructions were useless, written in a language resembling scrambled egg. At last it was done. Elvis lay on the sea-grass matting (Christ, she hated that sea-grass; she'd get a carpet, see if she wouldn't) under the tank. Bubbles rose in silence through the green water.

Moss ran upstairs and fetched her work lamp and angled it so that it shone down into the aquarium, catching all the pretty fish — a gleam here, a glint there — and through onto Elvis's face, cool, green, content, his eyes half closed, straw-coloured lashes against pale skin.

Moss went to the window, touched her avocado plant, which had never been the same since someone ripped the middle out of it, and looked out at her garden in the dying light. Something had bloomed during the day. Moss could never remember the names of things and Nicholas and Alexandra always carried off those lilting descriptive labels. Lovely, though. She opened the window. The cats sprang up onto opposite walls and faced each other with tails curved into question marks. Tea time.

'What shall we cook for tea, sweetie?' she asked. 'Eggs and chips or I could . . .' A snore interrupted her. She turned. Elvis. How funny that so small a boy should snore. His hands were folded together on the Fair Isle waistcoat Clarice had knitted him: it had real mother-of-pearl buttons. Moss had wanted her mother to knit her one too, but all Clarice had had to say to that was 'You're a big girl now,' a comment that had left her daughter inexplicably sad for days.

The fishy shadows deepened, moved along the walls. Moss sat on the floor beside Elvis, stroked the hair back from his forehead. He seemed more settled lately. A while ago she'd been worried when he'd disappeared for quite long periods, taking various household objects with him. That frightful ice-cream scoop for example, which she couldn't remember ever using, let alone how she got it in the first place. Moss had a certain sense of danger past and was grateful. She reached out her hand and softly touched the tip of his nose in blessing and request: please don't let him grow up too straight, or too boring, but just enough of each to prevent him being too unhappy.

The cats came in and stopped, stared and grew stealthy, circling this new thing.

Moss supposed there was no point expecting Hazel. Already she seemed to be not just out but gone entirely from the house. Moss found it difficult to decide whether she minded or not, which was not like Moss at all. If it weren't for the cats she could quite easily have gone to sleep herself, but she knew if she did they'd eat the fish and then there'd be a scene she couldn't even begin to imagine. She must see about getting a cover for the aquarium. Moss felt harassed as she got up to feed the cats. Then she had a gin and the evening settled into cheerfulness.

Later that evening Sue rang from Lyme Regis. Moss was pleased to hear from her. They chatted for a while. Moss told her about the aquarium. Sue said she'd like to see it one day when she was up in town. Moss said that that sounded like a good idea, trying to sound casual while her mind played idly with various erotic fantasies. It had been nice with Sue, and the first time too. Nonetheless, when Sue said goodbye and she'd hung up the phone, Moss felt more cautious. Nice is nice, but she hoped Sue wasn't going to attach too much significance to what had happened. The phone rang again.

'Surely not,' said Moss out loud, but it was only one of the mothers from the play group phoning to confirm that Elvis wouldn't be coming any more, was really starting nursery school next week because poor Fiona's mother had been waiting ages to get her into the group and was so thrilled that there might be an opening after all.

This random violence is a worry.

Why did what happened, happen?

Why him, why them, why you, why me and, in this case, why Renate?

The Bogeyman fusses some more with his lace cuffs and, finding they are not quite dry, leaves them where they are and clags off across the sticky brown lino in search of clues.

Since this otherwise unremarkable room is lined floor to ceiling with grey metal filing cabinets and card indexes he hopes to find something that will provide an explanation if not a defence because, though marginally brain-damaged, he is neither a fool nor notably mad and he does not expect to get away with this. He doesn't expect to be hung for it, either.

He looks for the light switch, composing headlines in his head. I BAKED MY DOG IN THE OVEN. No, that's not right. HOUSE OF HORROR. Dull, But better.

Scrabbling in a far dark corner alerted him that she was awake.

'Holy hell,' said the skinny witch, for it was she. 'There must be a way out of this fucking Gulag.'

Harold opened his eyes, and then closed them. 'You'll have to speak up,' he said, and wished he hadn't because he didn't want to hear anything she had to say. He returned to the concentration camp fantasy running in his head.

'You freaking psycho,' she muttered and crashed back to sleep. Five minutes later she woke again with something else to shout. Her words elbowed their way past his Guards: those cheerful volunteers drawn from the surrounding countryside. 'I was at Greenham,' she said. 'For a whole fucking year.' Harold thought that that explained a lot.

The Guards beat their ears in disbelief.

'Achtung!' they bellowed. Harold never had to ask the Guards to speak up. The Guards always came in loud and clear. 'Filthy lesbo.'

'You don't want to believe everything you read in the papers,' she said. But the Guards could not read. They knew what they knew and that was that.

She came and sat beside him, a move he did not welcome. She said her name was Sylvia. Who was Sylvia? What if she had a fit? He could feel her shivering. The Guards weren't cold; full of good rye bread smeared with goose fat, they stamped through the frozen furrows of his mind, each and every one of them brimming with the kind of health most aptly described as rude. The question was: who had planted them there? Harold was starting to understand. He may have lost a foot but he was beginning to find an answer.

'If I put my arms round you we'd both feel warmer.'

But Harold wasn't falling for any of that help-me-make-it-through-the-night crap. He preferred to take his example from the Guards.

'Raus!' he growled.

'You're nuts,' said Sylvia. 'You know that, don't you?'

Walter sat on the closed lid of the toilet in a suite at the Savoy watching Hazel in the bath. She'd said she could do nothing without having one first which, considering the condition she'd been in, was obviously wise. Her filthy socks lay on the floor.

He'd had a bit of trouble getting her into the Savoy looking like she did, but Walter had a way with minions. Now he wondered what on earth he was doing here. He'd never done this, not in all his twenty-four years of married life, so why start now?

Walter loosened his tie and examined his heart for clues to his adulterous intention. Anger. Was that it? Anger toward Daphne for shutting him so completely out of her grief, denying him the comfort of comforting? Anger didn't seem a very good reason for making love to somebody.

Hazel turned the tail of the gold-plated dolphin-headed hot-tap and continued with her song.

> 'The bell-hop's tears keep flowing.
> The desk-clerk's dressed in black.
> They've been so long on Lonely Street
> They're never going back . . .'

He wished she'd stop it and she did, her words gurgling away as she sank underwater to melt her spikey head into soft curls. Her face bobbed up at him pink and pleasing. She stretched her arms above her head and sank back into the steam. Her breasts flattened to almost nothing but an excited jut of raspberry-coloured nipples. Mundane. Raspberry nipples. Daphne could doubtless do better but, in the interests of accuracy, he didn't see much wrong with his description, but then he wasn't bloody Daphne, was he?

Once, in Geneva and not long after their wedding, he had come upon Daphne on a hotel terrace beside a lake boring as tin in the moonlight and paused to . . . what? To wonder at her, perhaps, for it had been wonderful to him to see her standing in her long white dress chatting to fellow guests beside a stone balustrade. Her words had drifted to him on the scent of roses.

The moon had broken in her glass as she'd raised it to lips blood-red by day, smudged black by night, fed by dark willing kisses. Smug lips acknowledging the guffaws of others as Walter, growing chill, had stepped from the shadows to claim her.

He wondered if Rupert had had a girl. He thought not, for if so he surely would not be so careless of his life.

Walter unbuckled his belt and eased forward a bit on the seat.

'Ouch!' said Hazel.

'What?' Alarmed. 'What's wrong?'

'Soap,' said Hazel. 'Soap in my eyes.'

'I see,' said Walter.

What should he do next? Uncertain fantasies formed and fainted in the steam. Should he get in the bath with her? Would he fit? The years hadn't been entirely kind in that respect. Walter wondered if he were not perhaps a prudish man. He never told dirty jokes and barely understood them when told to him by others. He did not value or admire one part of the human body above another. He was, he thought, unsuited to his purpose. He sighed, closed his eyes, leaving his hands at rest in his lap.

'"What I aspired to be, and was not, pleases me."'

'Browning,' said Hazel.

Pleased, Walter went to her. He leaned over the bath and kissed her, pushing his tongue deep and gentle into her mouth in the manner she'd liked that night when she'd raised her hips toward him under the trees in Battersea Park. He reached for a towel, helping her to stand before wrapping her in it and bearing her out of the bathroom, round several big stuffed armchairs and far too many tiny tables to be described as occasional and finally, nervous, to bed.

Albert and Benjamin, Felix and Felicity, Dominic and Daphne sat round the table doing their best to eat up their dinners. It was Daphne who abandoned the effort first, pushed her plate away, lit a cigarette.

'Mum,' wailed Felix.

'Please don't,' whispered Felicity.

'You'll get c-c-cer-cancer,' added Albert.

Dominic and Benjamin, being that much older, merely raised their eyebrows at each other. Benjamin got up to make coffee, clinking across the kitchen in the chains that circled his waist, ran between his legs and dangled below the curve of his buttocks. Why? wondered Daphne. Why on earth? Was it attractive? Male display? Who knew? Did he?

'Yeah, Mum,' snarled Ben, clanking the kettle down on the cringing hob, scraping a match to start a fierce flame under it. 'You'll get c-c-cer-cancer. And emphysema.'

At the table Dominic affected a sickening gurgle deep in his throat, began to croak and cough. Felicity wanted to kill him, but what was the use? Her best friend, Behnaz, said Dominic was an awful show-off, and Behnaz was right.

'And heart disease,' continued Ben.

Dominic leapt up, clutched his chest, staggered a few steps and collapsed in a heap at his mother's feet.

'It hurts,' groaned Dominic. 'It bloody does. Why didn't anyone tell me? I would've been good, I swear I would.'

'Pack it in, arsehole,' yelled Felix. 'You're making Felicity cry. Ice-cream, Mum — is there any ice-cream? I'd like some. Chocolate chip. When you're quite through killing yourself, of course.'

American, thought Daphne. Why did Felix sound like an American? They all did. More and more they did. Was it television? But they had no television. Walter wouldn't have one in the house, and quite right too.

'You're going to die, Mum, if you don't watch it,' said the persistent Benjamin who loved his mother a lot. 'You're going to die horribly — and all at the taxpayers' expense.'

Daphne felt herself grow crosser and crosser, except cross was not quite the word for it. Anger grew inside her. Daphne and the kettle boiled. She flailed in limitless anger, a sensation close to that of drowning, or so she supposed.

Felicity studied her plate and wished it was time for school, but school was a whole night away.

'Why shouldn't I?' Daphne muttered through clenched teeth, desperate to get them apart, to let the words come out. 'Why shouldn't I?' she bawled, which felt better. 'Why shouldn't I bloody well die at the taxpayers' expense? Rupert is. So why shouldn't I?' She pushed back from the table and advanced on her second son, held him pinned against the dresser by his chains. The family china shook. The silver jingled in its drawers.

'What would you rather the taxpayers spent their money on? Bombs perhaps? Missiles? Some horrendous great nuclear war that'd put an end to all your rubbish once and for all?'

'No, Mum,' said Benjamin.

Felicity let out a terrible howl, jumped up from the table and ran from the room. Albert, pale, rose to go after her.

'You sh-sh-shouldn't, Mer-mum,' he said, his stammer writhing inside him with distress, threatening to silence him forever. Oh God, thought Daphne, my fault, my poor lovely Albert, as he knocked her proffered hand aside. 'Fer-Fer-Fee- is very f-fer-fri-'

'-tened,' finished Felix though he knew he shouldn't finish his words for him, but sometimes it was that or hit him.

'Frightened,' frowned Albert. 'Of ner-nuke-nuclear war. She der-dreams about it.'

'Let me go, Mum,' said Benjamin.

'Cer-whack, cer-rash, cer-thump,' cried Felix. 'We talk about it at school. And I think Dad's an old fool,' he added, 'because that girl's a lez.' And he got up and left the house, going to the shop in the High Street that rented video movies to luckier boys than him, just to have a look.

Albert took a slice of cold treacle pudding from the fridge and went to see if he could persuade Felicity to come out from under her bed and eat it.

Daphne let go Benjamin's chain and sat back down at the table. Dominic offered her a cigarette. 'Sorry,' he said. Daphne shook her head, unable to look at any face.

'It's all right, Mum,' said Benjamin, though nothing had been since Rupert had fallen through the roof.

'Don't be silly,' said Daphne. 'You know very well it isn't.'

'Have it your own way,' said Benjamin, and he left too, taking Dominic with him.

Different, all so very der-different (stop it) from the home life of our own dear Queen, thinks Daphne as she sits at the table and tells herself off. She shouldn't have blown up like that. How could she? Children. They were only children. And the bomb. How could she have dragged the bomb into it? Of course it frightens them. One knows that. But one forgets.

Pick a card, any card. The Bogeyman plucks one out. Like all the others it measures six inches by four inches and is lined with pale blue lines. On it (neatly centred) are typed (in capital letters) these words:

TODAY I HAVE SEEN
THE ULTIMATE INCONSOLABILITY
AND INCURABILITY
OF THE HUMAN SOUL

So, thinks the Bogeyman, staggering successfully over the too hard words, So-ho-ho. Soul sister. He slips the card back in the box where he'd found it, leaving a rust-coloured fingerprint in each corner. Lucky for her he'd come along. If that's how she'd felt she was better off out of it.

Hazel sat in bed and fooled with the TV's remote control, trying to find a late-night movie, but all she kept on coming back to was Stephen Spender talking about W. H. Auden, which all seemed mightily beside the point to Hazel.

Walter thought he'd met that chap somewhere, at some literary do he hadn't been able to escape.

Hazel laughed. Hazel loved hotels. She picked up the room service menu. Walter watched her read it. They'd done it once and he wanted to do it again. He imagined Hazel wouldn't like that phrase, but in his day that's the way they'd put it. But he was happy just to watch as she turned down the sound and stretched for the phone and dialled. Her back was pale and smooth, delicately boned and not unlike that of his youngest son, the nape so frail and biteable.

He would like to examine her closely all over but he didn't quite know how to make her be still long enough. She didn't seem very interested in his body and he supposed this was just as well. Supposing her to have slept with so many people that the finer details had ceased to fascinate her, if indeed they ever had, he resigned himself to studying her surreptitiously.

Hazel put the phone down. What had she ordered? Whatever it was, let it include a decent bottle of claret.

'Nice face,' she said, getting up to go to the bathroom. At first he thought she meant his, but then he saw she'd stopped in front of the box and was referring to Auden, the old brute. Walter was uneasy. He examined the back of his hands and then turned them over to inspect the palms. He detected a slight tremor. Parkinson's disease, he thought. In the circumstances it seemed the very least he deserved. What was he doing here watching a strange woman limp across the carpet on her way to have a pee, when he should've been at home with his wife fretting over the fate of their firstborn. It was a very slight limp. He wondered how she'd got it. Hazel turned in the bathroom doorway.

'Accident,' she said sharply and went inside and closed the door and didn't come out again until the food arrived.

Later on she'd heard that Lark had left whatshisname with the bad back and bought herself a little truck and gone to live in some mountains. It could have been in Aspen. Hazel had wondered (if indeed it was Aspen) how it was that Lark could afford to live there. Then she'd heard that it definitely was Aspen and that Lark had gone there with this older woman who dealt discreet drugs and smelt of subtle punishments, strong wrists and razor blades, and who they'd both had a thing about, once. And then Hazel had heard that Lark had left that woman and had come down from the mountains and was now enjoying some measure of professional success.

Beulah and her Southern belle are dry-humping each other to pieces in a farther room. In the room next to that, the Southern belle's entourage, namely her secretary, her English nanny and of course the three little boys, are fast asleep. At least the latter three are. The secretary is only pretending, being all too well aware what is going on next door. Never mind. It had happened before. It would happen again. She'd ride it out. An unfortunate image, bringing to mind her wild mistress astride that booted Yankee bitch, her skirts all rucked in a mad flounce, rings on her fingers, bells on her toes, going hell for leather and ending in a rebel yell that'll likely bring the Savoy down round their ears when it comes. When it does, Melanie (whose real name is Lottie Mae but the Southern belle won't have it) blunders up and gropes through her suitcase for a valium. The English nanny stirs and says a word that sounds like 'Winifred'; it is a long moan of protest. The three little boys snuffle sweetly in their blankets. Lottie Mae is not fond of them: the three little pigs.

Hazel is holding a short silver fork from which an oyster dangles. She's about to eat it when normal service is interrupted to bring them a newsflash and she forgets.

A fat segmented grub of an astronaut steps from the safety of the mothership and floats like a starfish on the end of his lifeline.

'I'd like to do that,' says Hazel.

The astronaut raises one gloved paw and waves it.

'Hi Mom,' calls Hazel, who finds it hard to be quiet when she watches television.

The astronaut lowers his hand. It closes round the lifeline and tears it away.

'This is it, Good Buddy. The infinite vacuum. The big Hoover,' hoots the astronaut and somersaults backward into the void. The bright ribbons of his laughter stream in his wake, snap and leave him alone and free out there beyond the limiting reach of all that drove him to it.

'God,' says Hazel. The oyster drops unregarded between the sheets. 'Top that.' She switches off the television.

Walter sweats beside her. 'Nine stone,' he says, his voice strained, dreadful, not like him at all. 'I used to be. I do apologise. I used to play a lot of cricket. Perhaps that was it. My son, my eldest son that is, he weighed only nine stone as well, but still he landed with an awful thump.'

Hazel takes the tray which rests across their knees and sets it on the floor beside the bed. She pours a glass of the rather good claret she's ordered, hands it to him and waits.

Walter thinks of Rupert's lifelines, the tubing that invades his body, holding him pinned so painfully (for Walter feels there must be pain, though the nurses smile and deny it) to life. Walter sees a hand enter the picture, a hand (but not his surely, dear Lord, surely not) that takes each tube and breaks it, freeing his son to finish what he'd started.

What can he be thinking of? Walter knows the world is falling into madness. It is a popular theme, but he wants no part in its development. Walter prefers to hide beneath the sheets. He wants to sleep for a while and perhaps he does.

Hazel ferrets him out.

'Feeling better?' Her face hangs over him. She picks at the oyster squashed to his cheek. That smile again. And her hair, the fight taken out of it by bath and bed, the dark flop of it across her eyes. Walter knows now who it is she's like. A dark person. What Daphne calls 'good bones', high colour, the smile that admits nothing. And under the surface he knows it's there. The chip of ice in the heart.

Walter pulls the boy to him.

'Rupert,' he whispers as he turns and enters him, driving deeper, deep enough to leave no room for demons until his son must call out 'Stop' and push him away, but Walter won't be pushed. Walter presses on, determined to get to the heart of the matter, to wash the secret wound and never to fail his son in love again and he doesn't, completing his task and crying out 'I love you.'

'That's no excuse,' says Hazel, when she is able to say anything at all. 'Who's Rupert?'

Beulah stands not quite alone in the pre-dawn on a soccer pitch in Regent's Park while the lions roar and rumble in the zoo. Beulah fingers the Southern belle's silky drawers snuggled in the pocket of her trench-coat, fingers her neck which is circleted with what she calls hickies and what Buster, unimpressed, will call love-bites and juvenile.

Beulah's heart is roaring with the lions; glorious, defiant, trapped. Beulah turns a cartwheel.

A short man, bored and bloated, watches from the sidelines, rubbing at the chalk marks on the grass with a discontented foot. He cannot sleep, excited by thoughts of suicide in outer space. That's one lucky bastard they'll never drag back. He thinks of his own failed overdoses. He walks toward Beulah, placing one neat shoe in front of the other. Only on stage can he leap, let go.

Beulah has taken the Southern Belle's knickers out of her

pocket and put them on her head. The first she knows of his approach is his voice, nuzzling through the scented darkness.

'Are you in love or are they yours? Did you steal them from a clothesline or were they given to you personally?'

'Oh yes. Oh no,' mumbles Beulah, muffled by mouthfuls of silk. He reaches out and plucks the knickers off. 'Oh no. Oh yes,' stammers Beulah, completing her answers.

'Is she pretty?' He rubs the fabric between thumb and forefinger. 'Nice.'

'Uh huh.' Beulah is thinking of selling this story to a newspaper because he is, as she now sees, this very famous person.

'Who is she?'

Beulah wonders if she should tell. She thinks she shouldn't but she can't resist. He nods and considers matters a moment.

'I will wear them. At the Baltimore gig. Next Saturday. Tell her. It'll amuse her.' Beulah doubts this. He runs away from her across the pitch. On the other side he stops, turns back.

'Love is wonderful,' he shouts. 'While it lasts.' He shrugs. Draws a finger across his throat in a slashing motion. 'Good luck!' And vanishes in a shiver of shrubbery.

'Love,' says Buster glumly, crunching up her cornflakes in the dim dawn before the baby wakes. 'I should be very careful if I were you.' Meaning: careful of what you say to me who, for love of you, has sat worrying in this room with its dingy yellow wallpaper every lonely wrinkle and stain of which I've learned by heart. I'm a love expert, that's what I am, so watch it.

'Aren't you pleased for me?'

'No. I am not pleased.'

Beulah stands abashed; a great bumptious baby who's just bounced across the carpet and stuck her finger in the light socket. But perhaps Buster has misunderstood something somewhere. Beulah will try to explain.

'It won't affect us, babe. This can't touch what we've got together. It's just — well, it's just lust.' Beulah smirks and giggles at her luck, though she tries hard not to. She resists an impulse to grab the dreary Buster and bite her ears. 'I mean, I don't respect her or anything. Not like I do you.'

Buster smiled. 'You consider me the more worthy, do you?'

'Worthy. Yeah. Right. That's it.'

Buster's heart fell flat on its face. Worthiness might be a criterion in companionship but is rarely rated in romantic love, and romantic love is what she wanted, it being just that bit more exciting.

'Companionship,' Beulah was saying, 'companionship is the important thing.'

Buster thought of old age, of bed-pans and chamberpots, of someone to change your library books, keep the garden tidy and see you through. Old age. That was the hey-day of companionship, no doubt.

'That other stuff doesn't last.'

'Why start it then?' But Buster doesn't need to be told. In passion Beulah catches glimpses of immortality, and who is Buster to quibble at such joy? She just doesn't want her nose rubbed in it, that's all.

'I don't know if I've ever mentioned this, but I'm a person who bears grudges.'

'What do you mean?'

'I mean, I wish you hadn't told me. It might just have passed and then I'd never have known and things might have been all right, but as it is I'll never forgive you.'

'But I thought you'd want me to be honest. Didn't we always say we'd be honest with each other? Remember?'

Buster doesn't.

'Go to her. Go on. Get out of here. Go.'

How had things gone so far so quickly? Buster's all at sea and it's swim or drown, she knows that.

'She did ask,' Beulah says and realises the words aren't coming out loud enough and has to start again. 'She did ask — she did sort of suggest I go away with her. A short vacation. Just to see what this was all about.'

'I thought you already knew what this was all about. Love. Irresistible passion sweeping all before it, including me.'

'Well yes, but it's not serious. I mean, it might not be. We owe it to ourselves to find out, don't you think?'

The baby begins to cry. Buster feels like joining in on exactly the same high note of urgency that seemed to suggest the house was burning down, their very lives on fire.

'She's got this farmhouse in Tuscany. It's beautiful. We read about it in *Architectural Digest*, remember?' says Beulah who clearly never knows when to shut up.

'You lied to me, I think,' says Buster softly. 'As I remember, I was to give you stability, the baby, all that. In return you'd l-l- —' her tongue wobbled wildly, '— love me.'

'But I still do. We still can have all that. Security. A place to hang our hats. Companionship. I'd never desert you, babe. I just want a — a —.'

'Sabbatical? I don't think you've put in quite enough time for that. Let's just say you're quitting.'

'I'm no quitter,' yelled Beulah, stung to her bootstraps. 'You can ask anyone. Ask my Pop.' Though how that drunken old Irish stereotype has gotten in on this act Goddess only knows.

'Yes you are. You're quitting. You're leaving me, and the baby and, worse still, you're betraying the movement. She's the enemy. She's a founding member of Ladies against Women. And she'll never acknowledge you. You'll be locked in the attic: Mrs Superstraight with seven super-stud husbands to her credit and more to come no doubt and her three male children and worst of all those fat titillating books she churns out by the ton. Think what you'd do to her sales if you got out.'

But Beulah's beyond help. All she sees is Mrs Superstraight sprawled on sheets of messed up satin begging Beulah not to stop. Beulah wants to rush back to the Savoy and see about it.

'I respected you so much, Beulah.' Is Buster going to cry? They both hope not. 'Your work. What you did.'

'What I did.' Beulah's voice is flattened by the weight, the impossibility, of explaining these things to Buster.

What she'd done had been easy at the time. So easy to snatch attention, to be clever and quick and ahead of it all with smartasses like Mailer and Greer feeding you the lines. Easy to trash and yell and break things up. But times got colder and times got harder and in those times a strong desire to grab the world by its ears and turn it upside down hadn't been enough. It had been necessary to regroup, pay attention to detail, talk tactics, and become politicised, suck up to idiots and talk-show hosts, put in some heavy time, to write, to publish and to convert and Beulah had been unable to make the switch. She'd become bored, missed the flash, the trash, the attention of the old days and, it had to be said, the hit-and-run sex that went with them especially now when wherever you stuck your finger was fraught with significance.

But, worse than that, Beulah knew she was frittering away her time on picayune projects in this weary city no matter what Buster said about everything counting and it all adding up in the end. To hell with it. Beulah just wanted to be alone somewhere hot and scented and out of time with the Southern Belle and to hell with the whole freaking world which would spin on no matter what she, Beulah, did or did not do. Unless of course the boys dropped a bomb on it, but better not get onto that, thought Beulah, or I'll never get out of here.

'I'm going,' she said, and went.

Waking before dawn, Moss sat despondent on Hazel's bed; kicked crossly at the pile of overdue library books on the floor beside it.

Something had to be done. This just wasn't good enough, really. How much longer could Moss be expected to go on giving Hazel the benefits of all her doubts?

A wobbling thunder of a thousand voices.

> 'Oh, Canada
> The true north strong and free
> Oh, Canada we stand
> We stand on guard for thee . . .'

Coloured spots splashed a thousand faces, bounced along the ice in fragments. Patriotism gave way to frenzy as the opposing PeeWee teams tumbled onto the ice from opposite ends of the rink. Le Professeur de Judo rose to his feet. There she was, his Little Lucienne, last out of the tunnel, trailing her team across the ice to swoop in their wake during the warm-up circuits, a gaudy padded penguin darting past her father, footwork sure and neat.

Tomorrow he leaves for London to kill Hazel and Lucienne goes to Montreal. She is not pleased, fearing she'll be dropped from the team for missing practice. Le Professeur's sworn on his mother's life they'll be back in time for next week's game and the drama of his oath has persuaded her to believe him.

On the third circuit Lucienne slows, glides past him with her stick raised in the air, her other arm raised most firmly to the ringing roof, fist clenched. Behind the face-guard, sinister, silly, her eyes gleam with glee and her smile curves back at him, hangs on the thrilled air a second as she shoots away to take her place in goal.

Le Professeur de Judo slumps back in his orange plastic seat. He can't watch. He shuts his eyes against the spectacle of her being bruised and buffeted by those great brutes of boys. He grips the sharp edge of his seat to keep from making a fool of himself by rushing out onto the ice and banging all their heads together.

'Dreadful, isn't it? I can't think why I come. Well, I can, actually. It's Bernard.' A clear voice, English in its clarity. He opened his eyes. An expensive sheen of fur. She was a tall woman, her back to him, leaning forward over the safety barrier, frowning slightly at one of the gaily suited thugs on the opposing team. 'And the injuries. Why, last season Bernard . . .' she turned to smile at him, 'but I mustn't worry you, must I? Not with your daughter making her debut. They say she's awfully good. I follow these things, you see.' She sat down beside him. All along the rows beside and in back of them parents and siblings in team colours stamped and roared until the stadium walls shook. 'Awful, aren't they? Gross, as Bernard would say. George won't come. Refuses point blank.'

The teams streamed across the ice in streaks of colour, clashed and fell apart in rainbow tatters that he could not follow. He saw the hard black lozenge of the puck hurtle toward the home goal, heard the thud as Lucienne deflected from her pads, caught and controlled it with her stick and sent it whizzing safely away.

'You see. She's very quick. She's clever. Anticipates well. She'll be perfectly fine.'

'Yes.'

'Marian,' she said, offering what he recognised as being an elegantly gloved hand.

Le Professeur de Judo extended his own matted mitten. 'Paul.'

'That's good.' She said this briskly, as though something had been achieved. Then she turned her attention back to the game.

At half-time Paul followed Marian out to one of the bar areas in the concrete maze of corridors and exits wrapped round the inner core of the stadium.

She turned as he crunched up behind her over the peanut shells and candy wrappers, a bottle of Labatt's Blue dribbling in each hand. She handed him one of the cold slippery bottles and raised the other to her lips, tilting it briefly toward him as she did so.

'Cheers.'

'A votre santé,' he said and drank, forgetting for the moment how much he disliked this or any other beer.

'Born in the USA,' thundered Bruce Springsteen over the public address system. A slight movement of her mouth indicated her distaste at this piece of cultural imperialism. As a French Canadian such conceits coming from the anglophile red-necks who held sway round here usually made him walk away but, like the beer, it seemed he could overlook anything this evening.

This woman was, he thought, like no one else he'd ever seen. Or once, perhaps, he'd known people like her, before his life had closed down so completely and he'd ceased to see anything clearly. Well-groomed. Elegant. All such words applied. Ordinary, plain, unpleasing people like himself stood all about them clad in jeans, down jackets, running shoes.

'I like your sweater. It's a Cowichan, isn't it? A very fine one, I think.'

'Thank you. I bought it on the Island.'

'George is on the Island.' She wore soft boots with short slender heels. Her brown hair fell shining to her shoulders. Her greenish eyes looked rather serious at the mention of this George. 'Where do you live?'

'Point Grey.'

'That's very nice.'

'It's handy to the university.'

'Is that all?' she said and laughed. He wondered what was funny. Where did she live?

'Kamloops.'

He couldn't imagine her in Kamloops. He'd been there, he thought. He had some memory of slithering roads, of getting out in a blizzard just after Hell's Gate to put chains on the tyres and all the time Hazel had had her nose stuck in a book because she didn't like scenery much.

'In a fortnight's time your daughter's team is travelling up by bus for an exhibition game on Saturday afternoon. She could spend the night with us and you could drive up on Sunday to collect her. George has promised to be with us. Would you? If you're free?'

'Perhaps. I . . .'

'Another engagement?' She smiled. 'Of course.'

He wondered how she'd respond if he told her that by then he'd have dashed across the North Atlantic to murder his ex-wife because she was mad, bad and didn't like scenery.

'Paul?'

How could he have loved so unsatisfactory a person?

'I'll try.'

'Thank you.' Thank you? She was wonderful. What did she mean, thank you?

Marian crossed to the concrete parapet and looked down on the rink. He went and stood beside her. Together they stood and watched the giant roller being driven back and forth across the ice, restoring it in readiness for the second part of the battle.

Walter walks the streets for hours, bits of Browning bounding about his brain. He crosses Waterloo Bridge and, overcome with nausea outside the National Theatre, throws up into the Thames. Watching the water tear past his eyeballs at a great and greasy speed Walter realises that there is nowhere to go but home.

Daphne too must walk the streets but not just any streets, only those that lead to God. As she walks words keep her company, lend measure to her step. When she must stop to cross the road they slop against the boney confines of her forehead, flow over the inner ledges of her eyes. Seeing them so comically exposed she scribbles a balloon around them and reads them loudly and with relish.

'As it was in the beginning is now and ever shall be world without end Amen.' An elderly gentlman who also stands and waits and cannot bear to see a woman cry must give her his opinion.

'Surely,' he says and 'surely,' he repeats, 'there can be no more comfortless words in the entire language. Just look about you, madam, and take pause,' he woofs. 'The Bard would serve you very much better.' But Daphne does not hear him.

The elderly gentleman brandishes his furled umbrella at a passing taxi but it seems this is not his day to be noticed. Rather than have to hear Daphne run through the whole blessed thing again he rushes away and trips impetuously to his death under a No. 29 bus.

Daphne, perceiving a lull in the traffic, continues on her way.

The passengers spill onto the road, each instructing others to find phones and summon ambulances. The bus driver beats his steering wheel in distress and disbelief. The bus conductor kneels beside the body, removes his cap and places it respectfully over the elderly gentleman's face.

A young man who, having stepped out of the cake shop with the jam doughnut intended for his breakfast, has seen the whole thing runs after Daphne. Catching up with her, he takes her arm to stop her.

'Come back. It's your duty, you know. You're a Witness.'

'I certainly am not. I am a Roman Catholic,' she states, with the emphasis on the Roman. She has found before that this statement leaves all brands of religious fanatics with very little room to manoeuvre, and so it has proved again. She notes with pleasure that this particular pest is silenced.

But then, 'You've no sense of civic responsibility,' he calls after her. 'No heart,' he tells himself as he returns to the scene to wait for the police. 'None,' he says as he picks up one of the elderly gentleman's shoes which has landed on the pavement some yards away and then drops it again. He retrieves all the bits of broken brolly. He stands disconsolate and late for work. All he can think of is Humpty Dumpty.

Even in sleep the ghost of a 'we-won' smile haunted Lucienne's mouth. Having tipped her safely into bed, the number-one hockey stick tucked in beside her, her father was unable to do the same thing for himself.

He found himself walking round the apartment, picking up this thing or that, examining it as though he'd never seen it before, and putting it down. He thought of nothing in particular, his mind a relieved blank.

Their suitcases stood by the front door in readiness for an early departure.

He went to the kitchen, put a fresh filter in the coffee maker, put beans in the grinder so they'd be all ready to go at the touch of a button. Now what?

He picked up his keys from where he'd dropped them on the kitchen counter. A drive would be good, he thought. A nightcap at one of the bars on Davey Street; an option he quickly dismissed. He couldn't expose this fragile restless tranquillity to the pesterings of hookers and drunks, daren't let their displays of pain stir up his own.

In the cathedral Daphne makes mad pacts and promises. Daphne does not usually grovel to bleeding plaster saints but needs must when the devil drives. Driven, Daphne in her draggled dress, headscarf dense and paisley, kneels to make her frantic murmured rush of a promise viz: that if her eldest son should be restored to her in working order, or something very like it, then she, Daphne, will not whine if God in all his wisdom and glory ordains that she never write another word, not one.

Only once before has Daphne entered into such a negotiation, though with nothing like so drastic a promise attached. She evokes the moment now — a pastel impression of a younger woman in a dress with flowers on it and blue high-heels, she thinks. Yes, definitely blue shoes kneeling before the mother of God who also wears blue, though there is nothing on her feet as this seriously pretty young woman kneels in front of them asking only that the statue find her a party on this gorgeous soft and scented summer night; a party full of handsome clever people with nothing but sex on their minds.

Was this where she met Walter?

If so, three cheers for the Virgin Mary.

'What a cunt,' says the Bogeyman and reads the card again.

> ' "Love," he said, "is taking it out of your mouth
> and sticking it up your bum."
> "Yes," she said.
> "But true love," he said, "true love is taking it
> out of your bum and putting it in your mouth." '

What was this anyway? Her diary.

He'd spent the night probing the dense thicket of her tiny writing. It had been quite simple at first.

> 'Love means never having to say you're sorry.'

But things had grown more complicated as she'd warmed to love's complexities. He wondered why she bothered writing about all this. Why didn't she just buy the video? There were lots about, several providing all the activities described on that card.

' "Love makes the world go round," ' quoth the Bogeyman. What about that then? That was one she'd missed.

Le Professeur de Judo pads through a light drizzle round the muddy path that circles Beaver Lake, his footfalls thick with leaves.

The moon shines behind the pines. Out in the lake the beavers clunk and thunk, moving their logs about, rearranging their dam. They move the water with their big flat tails, leaving the lily-pads

102

slapping in their wake.

As he walks le Professeur thinks with pleasure of his mother's beef bouillion with lots of golden croutons bobbing about in it. On this particular occasion he has been unwell — not seriously so, some childhood malady involving fever, vomiting, loss of appetite — but now he was better and hungry again and she brings him a cup of this bouillion on a small, lacquered tray, and nothing from that day to this night has ever tasted better, filling him with warmth and life, pouring down his throat like hope renewed. He can feel it now, this hope renewed, this warmth, this reopening of possibility. And why? Because of meeting Marian, the possibility of a new love? No, not that (think of George).

It is this business of forgetting; the bliss of that. Being free of his obsession with his busted love for five, ten, fifteen minutes at a time.

The beavers chuckle in their dam. The moon still shines behind the pines. He hears the beavers. Sees the moon. His ears, eyes, mouth and sanity are his again.

All that remains is for him to take that gun and throw it out over the reeds where it revolves once butt over barrel and splashes down into the deepest part of the Lake.

Le Professeur de Judo doesn't stop to watch.

He is hungry. He is headed for Davey Street, to a bar he knows where he can get a club sandwich, cognac and coffee because nobody's pain can hurt him now. He turns on the car radio. Mozart's second violin concerto wraps itself around his heart. Aah! It's not that he no longer expects to feel the pain of her loss. He knows it will come again. But now he knows that it will pass, that the long time of falling and calling her name out is over.

Paul tears up his airline ticket and feeds the pieces one by one to the night winds.

The Bogeyman is hungry too. He can hardly be otherwise with that great greedy eel of misery writhing in his gut. It can never be otherwise, due to his unwanted, undernourished status from the word go. That is the theory anyway, but how to quiet it?

He goes to the fridge. He takes out the big plate on which

Renate's breasts sit side by side. He slaps the frying pan on the stove and pours in some oil.

Well, you never know. It might work.

Walter and Daphne approach each other with caution around the curve of the crescent. They stand looking at each other in front of the tall gate set in the stone wall above Daphne's sunken garden. Then he opens it that she may enter.

'You didn't come home,' she says.

'I'm home now,' he replies.

Daphne pushes past him. The wooden soles of her Doctor Scholl sandals smack smartly against the bottoms of her feet as she descends the steps. Her dress lightly brushes the crumbling brickwork releasing the stinging scent of the thyme which clings to it. Neglect is a word that comes to mind but that's enough of that, thinks Walter. There'll be no more neglect, he promises, followering her round the sundial where the honeysuckle twines, past lavenders and buddleias and along the path past the old stone wall where foxgloves lean together in the narrow shade and then through the sliding glass doors and into the house.

She pulls off her paisley scarf and drops it on this morning's *Times* untouched upon the table.

She walks across the kitchen, through the pantry and up the short flight of stairs leading to the front hallway. She turns to face him among the serious wine-gum colours flung down from the stained-glass fanlight with a saint on it above the front door.

She has nothing to say to him, but he has lots to say to her, beginning with 'I love you,' his lips and chin cast purple by the extraordinary light.

Daphne shakes her head, blue-green and beautifully shaped.

She bends to scoop the post from the mat, sorting through it with hands attributable to the Umbrian school. Bills and an aerogramme from her aunt in New Zealand and a postcard from their neighbours Jane and Simon who are in Ibiquera researching a book.

'I hate these things. They always end in bits no matter what you do to them.'

'I know.' He takes the aerogramme from her and lets it flutter floorwards to land in a puddle of pink. He finds he wants to put his arms round her. On top of that he's itching to tell her about the necessity he feels of fostering in his children a sense of order, the historical continuity he most strongly believes in, especially after his disquieting night with Hazel, but perhaps this wasn't the time. And that frightful business with the astronaut. It preyed on his mind. Surely he'd dreamt it? If not, it would be in the *Times*. He'd have a look later.

'You spent last night with a lesbian,' said Daphne. 'Felix told me.'

'Felix watches too much television.'

'We don't have television. And even if we did I find such programming most unlikely. Lesbians love the Savoy. They get dressed up and go there in droves. It gives them that sense of tradition they so sadly lack,' said Daphne, making things up as is her habit.

'I needed to think. I think best in traditional surroundings. Though they've tarted it up terribly. Arabs, I expect.'

'Or lesbians,' said Daphne darkly. 'Were you alone?'

'Not entirely. There was a room-service waiter.'

'Were you unfaithful to me?'

'My taste doesn't lie with waiters. I'm worried about Felix, you know. That was an odd thing to say. I'd better have a talk to him. Though he's a tight-lipped little sod, don't you think?'

'He can be. When it suits him,' she said. Her own lips were trembling. 'They send women to men in hotel rooms, even at the Savoy. Tell me the truth. Yes or no?'

'Is it that important to you?'

'Of course it is. And don't lie. I can always tell.'

Walter dismissed this for the nonsense it was.

'No,' he said.

The psychiatric social worker ties up his bicycle and admires his mural. Smoke pours out of the upstairs window at the back of the house. Max the Alsatian moans in the gutter. Funny.

The psychiatric social worker opens Eric's door but Eric isn't there. He goes to the foot of the stairs.

'Renate,' he calls and then, 'Renate?'

There's a smell of a type he's not smelled before and in his line of work he comes up against a lot of ethnic cooking.

The psychiatric social worker climbs the stairs.

The doors of the service lift came together with a rubbery sigh. So far so good. Hazel had seen a lot of interesting things as she'd wandered round the hospital in the white coat she'd borrowed from the locker room in the basement.

She'd been asked for and had given her opinion on a number of important things. It wasn't hard. She'd found she had a flair for it.

She didn't know the number of the room Rupert was in but she did know what floor. She pressed the round button with 7 written on it.

Oh God oh shit oh no oh dear.

'Boo,' says the Bogeyman looking autumnal and oddly jolly in his russet suit of dried blood.

She'd supposed a person in a coma would look peaceful, attractive even, along the lines of the Sleeping Beauty, but Rupert lay like a boy crucified, his emaciated limbs arranged in a manner that supported the comparison. He was pierced in many places by needles attached to tubes attached to machinery attached to a plug in the wall. Last night Walter had spoken of this plug and then: 'This'll all seem like a bad dream in the morning,' he said. But it didn't, thought Hazel, not really.

She went to the window and looked out over the Common, her hands deep in the pockets of her borrowed white coat. Council workers in Day-Glo orange jackets were dismantling the newly restored bandstand, carrying it away in pieces and loading it on the back of a lorry parked on the path in front of the café.

A tall man, gaunt and handsome, was entering the room but Hazel did not notice because she was puzzling about the bandstand and worrying about endings.

Hooper went to Rupert's bed and sat on it.

'You knew I'd come back, didn't you, you poor little wanker? You knew I wouldn't let you down.' Hooper nestled amongst the tubes and instruments, taking Rupert in his arms. He placed his ear against Rupert's throat, was the only one in the world to catch his small assenting mew. 'That's all right then,' he murmured, kissing him gently on his straining eyelids, his poor cracked lips. 'When you're ready. There's no hurry.'

There's only one ending, thought Hazel, always ever only one. Everything in between was only plot and sometimes, engrossed in the plot, it was easy to forget the inevitable ending which, she supposed, was the only point in having a plot at all lest everyone crack up and exit without permission somewhere between point A and point B.

On the bed Rupert clutched Hooper and then relaxed and let him go. Quietly Hooper reached out his arm and pulled the plug and so, when Hazel finished brooding by the window and turned to do the job she'd come to do, she found that it was already done.

Sylvia the skinny witch was trying to see through the illusion of self and time to the great oneness and suchness of being but all she could see was the fence.

'Why do they call themselves the Kali Kosmic Konsciousness?' asked Harold.

'Well, they could hardly call themselves General Motors, could they? Besides, they love all that Kali carry on.'

'What carry on?'

'In the yurt. They paint their faces red and their tongues black and hang monkey skulls round their necks and fuck, mostly.'

'I never knew that.'

'I know. You didn't give them enough to entitle you to fringe benefits.'

'I gave them all I had.'

'Quite,' said Sylvia.

'How do you know so much?'

'I get about. I listen at keyholes. I've been to the yurt.'

'There must be more to it than sex.'

Sylvia raised her hand and ticked them off on her fingers. 'One, there's money, two, there's Armageddon, and three, the KKKs will inherit the earth provided they've paid their deposit. What's the matter?'

The Guards are marching back from breakfast, egg on their ties.

'They've got their own nuclear weapons stashed all over the world and they've got KKKs in the military services of all the major nations in case the government lets them down and they have to start Armageddon all by themselves.' She leaned over and whispered in his ear but the Guards picked up on it nonetheless. 'We've got to get out of here, Harold. Warn the world what they're up to.'

The Guards, who knew a thing or two about the world and what moves it, sniggered and stuck their fingers up their noses.

'Moon Baby III will be here soon to look at your stump. I'll overpower her and then we'll run away. I'll carry you or something. We'll manage.'

The Guards exchange scowls, seize Harold's arms and drag him back to 1945 and set him down just inside the gates of Belsen next to one Sergeant-major Birtwhistle who, to compensate for his round youthful face, has carefully built himself the reputation of being exceptionally loud and officious even for an NCO. Not only that. This morning Sergeant-major Birtwhistle has exceeded himself entirely by arriving here ahead of the Americans, for whom he was supposed to wait. Now he wished he had. Sergeant-major Birtwhistle is silent, quivering inside, totally abashed at what he now must see. The Guards are not abashed. The Guards have always enjoyed an audience.

One thing Birtwhistle does not see (being happily bound to one time and one place) is his son Harold standing beside him, because of course his son Harold is at this moment busy being born in a granite labour ward in Aberdeen, Scotland, where Sergeant-major Birtwhistle's wife has been sent to escape the bombing.

What Birtwhistle does see standing next to him is this gape-

mouthed toothless skeleton dressed in a pyjama top and all lop-
sided due to the loss of his foot, swollen genitals dangling like
some grotesque and deadly growth down past the knees. In a
panic lest it touch him, Sergeant-major Birtwhistle lashes out and
knocks it down. It lies like broken twigs and then it starts to crawl.

Harold crawls, beats hard upon the boots of the Guards with
skinny fists, begging to be taken home.

'But you are home, Harold. Have you not always felt homeless
in the world? Out of step and all alone as you picked your way
through the wrecked landscape of your post-war post-industrial
childhood, watched the only one in the world to love you
unconditionally die a death by any standards horrible, were
married to that ball-breaker and finally forced to seek your destiny
amongst the savage heathen? Well, look no further, Harold. This
is it. Everything else was a pale imitation.'

Soldiers are entering the huts and coming out again pale and
puking. One falls to his knees, waves his rifle at the sky and cries
out against a God that allows these things to go on. In the granite
labour ward of the Aberdeen General Hospital Rita Birtwhistle
cries out too and with much the same protest in mind. The doctor
dashes pepper in her face. One good sneeze should do it. This
is an old Scottish trick. The doctor stands back as Mrs Birtwhistle
takes a deep breath. Sergeant-major Birtwhistle roars with rage.
The Americans will be here soon, rolling above it all in their tanks.
It will not do to have them find his men weeping and wailing like
women over man's inhumanity to man. To set an example
Birtwhistle yanks the skeleton to its foot. He wants it to stand, but
it won't. He tells it it is saved, but it won't listen. It seems intent
on hanging itself from the brass buttons of Birtwhistle's uniform.
Birtwhistle flings it from him. This time the skeleton does not
tumble but hops away toward the perimeter fence. 'Stop,' screams
Birtwhistle. 'Stop! Stop! Stop!' The skeleton reaches the wire,
hooks its talons as high as it can and drags itself upward. Once.
Twice. A bit further. And no more. It dangles motionless on the
wire. Then it lashes, thrashes, arches outward in a terrible spasm
and dies. A soundless scream catapults across the cosmos,
ricochets around a bit, transforms itself into a splendid bellow and
lands plop in the mouth of Mrs Birtwhistle's baby as it pops its

head out from between her legs in the granite labour ward in Aberdeen, Scotland.

'It's a laddie,' declared the doctor, 'a bonnie baby boy with all his wee parts in place.'

'I'm a cosmic mistake,' gasps Harold as they tie up Moon Baby III. And later as they stagger across the garden like ill-matched competitors in a three-legged race. 'My soul belongs to somebody else. It ricocheted across the universe and crash-landed in Scotland during the war.'

'Like that poor old bugger Hess,' pants Sylvia. 'And look how far that got him. Now stop talking. Save your strength for the fence.'

'I'm going to die on that fence,' says Harold happily. 'It's pre-ordained. Then I'm coming back as myself.'

Sylvia loses her temper and drops him.

'Crap Harold. That's crap. You're not a lost soul. What you are is mad. You are mad because your brain chemistry is fucked up. It has nothing to do with intergalactic error, or your Dad, or the Nazis or anybody else. One day, Harold, there will be a pill that mad people like you can take and that'll put a stop to more rubbish than you can shake a stick at including religions both organised and disorganised, UFOs, Armageddon and — oh shit Harold, come on. They're coming.'

Harold gets up, hops hard toward the fence.

'You'll see,' says Harold cheerfully.

Walter and Daphne make their good married love at the foot of the stairs, spattered by Godly colours. A person ultimately known as Dimity is conceived. Dimity, being so late and blessed a child, is sweet, biddable and never quite right in the head. It is reassuring to them both to know that she will never aspire to any heights and thus will never fall from them.

What's that noise? Oh Jesus no. The bastards. They've turned on the power. Harold dangles on the perimeter fence, a single coil of blue smoke rising in an eternal question mark from the top of his head. Sylvia, who'd made it over the fence ahead of Harold (though she'd tried to help, had pushed and shoved but he'd insisted she leave him and go on so she had), can see them all running across the no-man's-land behind the fence to pluck their trophy from the wire. What can she do? She can run, that's what she can do and she does. The helicopter rises from the croquet lawn. She won't get far.

Harold is taken from the wire and borne ceremoniously to a quiet spot on the river where he is disposed of in what the Lady Eleanor assures them is the Tibetan manner. The method is not at all offensive (she says) if it is done correctly and with respect and so they cut Harold up, roll each piece in barley flour and feed him, with as much respect as nausea allows, to the eels.

That evening the Leader summoned everyone to the yurt. Those who couldn't fit inside sat outside on the lawn while the Leader's voice crackled down on them from speakers in the monkey-puzzle trees. He comforted those that needed it. He rejoiced in the increased community strength and spirit that the young martyr Harold had brought to them. His soft padded hands described circles in the air. He spoke of the ancient sacred ritual of disposal they'd all had a hand in, how it symbolised the oneness and suchness and wholeness of being.

Not only that, thinks the Lady Eleanor as she sits playing with his plump and powdered feet on the silk-covered podium, it has the advantage of leaving absolutely no trace.

The skinny witch who'd said her name was Sylvia sits in the turret in chains until Moon Baby III, who's tired of all this, lets her out and drives her home.

'It's sad,' said Buster, 'don't you think?'

'Sad is a word I never use,' lied Moss. 'Though I used to when I was younger.' And thinks: I don't care if Beulah's bolted to Tuscany with a writer from the Deep South well-known and well-rewarded for her thinly veiled descriptions of the chronic repetitive sex lives of the straight and famous. I want to go shopping.

'She's got this farmhouse,' said Buster, referring to the above. 'She's got this farmhouse and I've got nothing.' She burst into tears. The baby strapped to her back did the same. Oh God.

'Could you get it through your nose,' asked Elvis who'd been under the table all the time reading *Spare Rib's* report on AIDS, 'if someone stuck their thing up it?'

The baby chewed the old 'SPERM KILLS' button pinned to Buster's lapel.

'The baby's eating your badge, Buster.'

Buster's hand went to the small dry scab on her forehead. She worried it with her finger.

'Don't do that,' said Moss, though the last thing she wanted with Buster was to play mother, 'you'll open it up again.'

'Sorry,' said Buster quickly, and sat on her hand. 'I didn't mean to be so personal. I just thought . . .' Her voice trailed away, defeated.

The two women sat looking at each other. Moss hoped there was nothing more to say, but she knew very well there was. She looked at the floor to avoid Buster's anxious eyes; Buster who used to be so full of herself.

Moss thought of one pouring morning last year when Buster had come to get something. She'd stood in the doorway while Moss had looked through a pile of her papers on the kitchen table to find whatever it was Buster'd said she wanted and suddenly Buster had been standing closer behind her, had slid her arms round her waist and turned Moss to her and kissed her and they'd ended up on the floor, Moss crying out with her jeans down round her ankles while Buster went down on her and wouldn't stop until Moss couldn't come any more and lay laughing, happy to find her ordinary morning so unexpectedly startled into pleasure. Then she'd pulled Buster up, kissed her and, tasting herself on the other's mouth, had grown excited all over again. She'd wanted Buster to stay. Wanted them to go upstairs to bed and spend the morning there. Buster had leaned over Moss, looking intently down into her face as though she'd lost something there.

'I didn't mean to do that.' Some other words had hung unspoken.

'I'm glad you did. Elvis is at play-group. I needn't pick him up

till lunch-time.' Moss had reached up, ran a quiet finger down
Buster's cheek. 'I'm crazy about you.'

'No,' said Buster, getting up. She stood over the half-naked Moss
looking angry. There was fear there too, but no time to work out
why. 'I've got to meet Beulah. I'm already fifteen minutes late.
That's quite enough time to keep her waiting, don't you think?'

Moss hadn't known what she'd thought. Buster was blaming her
for something. It had sounded like that. She'd felt stupid; hurt as
Buster, iron-clad and treading heavily as was her habit, had walked
to the door, where she turned and smiled at last on Moss.

'You shouldn't wear those jeans, you know. They've got this
irresistible little hole just . . .' Buster's hand had pointed to a spot
high on the inside of her own thigh '. . . there.'

'What?' But Buster had been out the door and gone. She'd
stopped to use the lavatory on her way out. Moss had stayed on
the floor and listened to it flush. She'd imagined Buster in there,
tidying her already tidy tight merino clip in the round mirror
above the hand-basin, squirting breath freshener down her throat.
The front door had opened, closed. The car had started out in the
street. Gone. Then had come another sound, a startling sobbing
which filled the kitchen and had nothing to do with pleasure.
Moss had hated to hear it but knew she wouldn't be able to stop
it for a while because it hurt. You didn't expect to be handed that
sort of macho bullshit by your sisters.

'I'm sorry the Collective had to break up,' Buster was saying
now.

'I'm not. We none of us has the energy for it any more.'

'I did,' said Buster, which was true. 'I sort of feel —' She blew
small trails in the soft hair of the baby's head, 'feel you all decided
things behind my back.'

Yes, they had. Not intentionally. Buster just hadn't been around
when it happened, that's all. Moss could understand how she felt,
but she didn't want to talk about it. Once, discussion would have
been imperative but now Moss just felt wrecked, exhausted by
what felt like a thousand years of talking with other women,
of listening, sharing and struggling to define their common
experience. It had been exciting, necessary, valuable, but now she
wanted to hand over the baton and let others — younger, stronger

113

women — continue the race. Moss knew this defeatist line would cut no ice with Buster, though the sporting metaphor might appeal. Moss tried to think of something to say that would prevent further discussion. She saw an article Hazel had torn from the *Guardian* and stabbed on the wall with the paring knife. Yes. That would do nicely.

'Besides,' says Moss, her voice falling and softening in an effort to strike sweet reason, the tone of one persuading a dog to give up its bone, 'wouldn't you honestly say, Buster, that we've all moved on a bit from the early days of the Collective? That indeed, darling, we may have reached a plateau beyond all that. Entered a sort of — uh, a sort of — um, post-feminist phase?'

Buster's eyes blurred behind a film of pain.

'You don't mean that. You can't.'

Just for a second Moss saw the other iron-clad Buster, last year's model, standing in the doorway telling her all about her irresistible hole, but that had nothing to do with what was happening now, did it? She whisked Elvis up from the floor and stuck him on her knee for protection. He resisted being used in this way.

'Stop it,' he said, taking a handful of her hair and pulling it. Ashamed, she let him go.

'I do mean it. And I'm not alone in my opinion, you know. It's a reasonable analysis.' Moss turned her guilty gaze to the bit of the *Guardian* curling on the wall.

Buster's lips essayed a curve of gentle understanding. Moss breathed a bit easier. Not for long. Buster leaned across the table, took Moss's hand, held it tight. 'And what,' she murmured, 'what does *Private Eye* have to say on the subject? What's their deeply reasoned analysis, lady?' She jabbed her nails into Moss's palm, hard enough to leave marks.

Buster's face closed; she packed it away and stood up to do the same with the baby. Buster was leaving; going to Berlin perhaps where, it was said, interesting things still happened. But first Moss must ask Buster if her baby's a boy or a girl. Buster's not forthcoming.

'The baby's perfect,' was all she said.

Moss saw Buster and the perfect baby to the gate.

'Ciao bella,' said Moss for old times' sake.

'Adios,' said Buster firmly.

Moss watched her trudge up the street to the bus-stop. She thought her brave. Buster stopped when she reached the corner and looked back at Moss. The baby's head poked from its pack, bobbed from side to side like a balloon. Traffic fumes blurred the line of trees growing at the edge of the Common across the busy road behind them. The whole scene felt wavery, uncertain, as did Moss's stomach as she raised her hand to wave goodbye.

'Good luck,' she cried, though by now Buster was far too far away to hear her. Moss noticed a strand of mauve wool caught on the gate post. As far as Moss could see, it ran all the way up the street. Buster had been wearing a mauve jumper. Was Buster unravelling?

Also: if this woman Beulah had run off with was so rich, why had Beulah found it necessary to take Buster's car with her? Life was full of loose ends.

From her vantage point up a tree Hazel watched Buster and the baby board the bus. Hazel couldn't stand Buster. Never could. Never would. Never had. Because Buster had been good at school. Because Buster's date and bacon scones never went up in flames during Domestic Science classes. Because Buster was a sneak. Because Buster had been crowned Miss Blue Gum Queen. Because Buster had been a Marching Girl and therefore ought to be shot. And, to top it all, Buster had had this perfect mother who made herself useful, a mother any girl could be proud of.

After that scene in the launderette, Hazel had hoped Buster might have forgotten the finer details of her own disastrous parent, but when she'd come home that night from watching Walter's house and opened and read the letter Buster had written and shoved under the door addressed to Moss, Hazel had known she hadn't.

It had all been there: all the old bad things. Hazel had wanted to cry, but found she couldn't. She'd torn up the letter but had been unable to do the same with her memories. They kept re-forming, re-focussing in clear colourful pictures. Mum's mad movie was up and running and its star, her lovely hair streaming free, looked briefly back at her daughter before turning back to watch the road, one hand on the big steering wheel all the cars had in those days, the other waving languidly at everyone she passed. Was she laughing? Had she ever laughed; had she perhaps felt free and happy as she drove those red dirt roads round Goondiwindi that take you nowhere worth going? Driving half dressed in Dad's ute with its hand-made bumper sticker reading JESUS WAS A FETUS (sic) TOO.

But one day Mum had been brought back by the cops. Drunk they said. Mum had accused these cops of beating and fucking and doing oral sex to her in a holding cell at the back of the station and Hazel had wanted to die of shame, only it had been Mum who died with her head in the gas oven and her feet in her neat white bowling shoes sticking out into the room, this being Mum's final rude comment on Dad's suggestion that she stop acting up and find herself a decent interest. Only, Mum being Mum, she'd managed to get each shoe on the wrong foot.

On the bus Buster unpacks the baby and examines her.

What could she have been thinking of just now, telling Moss that she'd been left with nothing, when all the time she had the baby. It would be Beulah who'd end up with nothing, discarded by the Southern belle and with a few or even several nights of bliss to show for it, and to what end?

After all, reasons Buster, busily knitting mental egg-cosies to sit on people's feelings to keep them nice and tidy, what person, when on their death bed, remembers an orgasm they had twenty years ago?

A baby, though — a baby would be different. You'd certainly remember a thing like that and find some comfort in it.

She really must think of a name for this baby. Something reaching back to the pre-patriarchal glory and yet, at the same time, heralding the bright dawn that lay in the future.

The baby raises its sea-anemone fist.

There is a seething in the sedge.

The Goddess of All Things rises roseate from the duck pond

116

to shine naked above the astonished Common. Gaia, Yemaya, Spider Woman, Ishtar or Ashtoreth and Demeter too come to crowd round Buster on the bus.

'Welcome to our world, Lamasthu, little lion-headed daughter of heaven.'

And the little lion-headed one smiles a smile that staggers the beat of her mother's heart.

The bandstand's gone.

The children's playground has been packed up.

Council workers advance on the trees with chainsaws. Is the Common being demolished?

Hazel slides down from her tree. She waits for a gap in the traffic. When it comes, she dashes across the road and finds her mother draped across a pillar-box raising and lowering her arm, beckoning Hazel down into darkness like poor Captain Ahab lashed to the back of the great white whale. Hazel doesn't know what to do. She falls to her knees filled with fright and remorse.

'Oh Mum,' she says, 'how could I?' How could I have sided with the cops? And, for that matter, how could I have sided with Dad against you, me of all people, because, believe me, Mum, I've found out just like you did how difficult it is to find a decent interest in life. 'I'm sorry, Mum,' wails Hazel. 'Forgive me.'

'I'm sure she will, ducks,' says this old man who's struggling to post a letter. He holds a white bull terrier by a steel choke-chain attached to a strap of plaited leather and is always kind to those in trouble. 'But I don't think praying to a pillar-box will do you very much good.'

'But I wasn't praying,' protests Hazel. 'I was just talking to . . . it was my mother . . . She was . . .' But not was, is. Mother has not gone.

'I must tell you,' spits this pillar-box, 'that I've always found your personal life disgusting. Even when you were little, you were at it.'

'And I must tell you,' says Hazel, getting to her feet and coming to her senses, 'that my personal life is my own affair and you must like it or lump it.'

'Of course she must,' says the old man, fishing in his pocket. 'Have a biscuit.'

'It tastes disgusting.'

'Rover likes them.'

Hazel is forced to stop half way down the street and be sick in Mrs Fisher's buxus which grows in a pot chained to the railings.

Hazel wonders why her mother never told her anything useful like the dangers of taking questionable biscuits from strangers.

Back to the kitchen where Moss is trying to find out why Elvis is crying so bitterly and won't speak and won't be comforted. She knows it has something to do with the *Evening Standard* because all he will do is wave it about and sob. At last she persuades him to give it her.

' "HOUSE OF HORROR", ' she reads.

'Sssh,' screams Elvis and climbs up on the table. 'He'll hear you and he'll eat you up too.'

Moss reads the front page to herself. About this man who's cut up a girl and eaten certain of her parts.

This is enough to make anyone cry, but worse yet is Elvis's insistence that this person, this Eric someone-or-other, used to live down the road and is, in fact, his father.

'But we don't know anyone called Eric,' protests Moss, knowing this is weak but it's all she can think of for the moment.

'Not Eric,' sobs Elvis. 'He's the Bogeyman, and he's been here all the time.'

'But sweetheart, darling, precious, listen. There's no such thing as the Bogeyman. It's just a thing stupid people say to make little children do what they want them to do.' Who'd done this to him? Her mother? She'd kill her.

'But there is,' insisted Elvis, pounding the paper with his fist. 'It's him. He's the Bogeyman, or else why's his picture in the paper?'

'Because he did this very bad thing and people are interested in this thing that he did.'

'But if he did this bad thing he must be the Bogeyman.'

'Not necessarily.'

118

'It's him. It's the Bogeyman and he's my Dad and he's coming to get me. He said he would. He said one day I'm coming back to get you, son, and then he ate up all the jam and went to sleep, only now he's awake and he's coming,' wailed Elvis and fell off the table. Moss fell after him, jarring her knees and bumping her funny-bone on the door knob, but she managed to grab him and hold him.

'Have I ever lied to you?'

'I don't know.'

'I've never lied to you, Elvis.'

'Okay.'

'This man is not your Daddy. I've got a picture of your Daddy in my bedroom.'

Moss and Elvis climb the stairs side by side and hand in hand, which is squashed, but they both feel better that way. Moss takes a wedding photo out of her drawer and gives it to him. She kneels beside him. He sobs and hiccups, and she finds she loves him so much she doesn't know what to do for him and probably never will.

'See?'

'Can I have it?'

'Of course you can have it.'

Elvis continues to examine it. 'You look like hippies.'

Moss takes the picture from him. 'Yes. We do.' It had been an outdoor wedding. Harold had wanted it held on his father's old allotment that someone else had taken over long ago and tarted up. In those days Harold's hair was thick and curly, falling to his shoulders. Afterwards they'd strolled with their guests down to the canal and gone away on one of those brightly painted barges. The canal was lovely round there; the tow-path sprinkled with confetti, champagne corks popping.

'Can we take it down the High Street and get it put in a nice frame?'

'This afternoon.'

'Mum?'

'Yes, Elvis?'

'You really sure there's no such thing as the Bogeyman?'

'Absolutely sure.'

'You've killed it, you filthy girl,' cries Mrs Fisher from the street. Elvis looks at his mother and his mother looks at Elvis.

'Only one person can get Mrs Fisher all wound up like that,' says Elvis, and he's right.

The front door bangs and Hazel's home.

'I'm leaving.'

'I know you are.'

'I'm sorry.'

'So am I.'

'We should talk about it.'

'Not now. Another time, but please not now. I can't.

But there was to be no other time, it seemed. Hazel was going home. Moss was surprised, considering how scathing she could be about the place.

'They say it's nowhere near as awful as it was. They've changed the government or something.'

Moss thought that sounded a feeble reason. It wasn't as if Hazel came from Chile or any of those places where governments carried clout and a change in one might cause people to go flocking back in gratitude.

Reserving the truth as a last resort, Hazel tries another tack.

'When was the last time you tried going to the beach around here?'

Going to the beach was an ambition Moss had not entertained since childhood and she thought that was as it should be.

'The sea's all filthy,' said Elvis. 'It's full of oil and toilet rolls.'

Hazel came clean and Elvis came close and listened.

'I want to say goodbuy to my mother. Take her flowers.'

It sounded like a fairy story. It had a road cut out of rock in it. This road wound round the side of a hill to a bleak graveyard which faced away from everything living. This is where Hazel had to go to find her mother. Hazel explained that this place was hard to find and that she would have to ask directions. She hoped her flowers would not all be dead by the time she got there.

'Your mother was always a difficult woman,' said Moss.

Elvis, puzzled by mothers, nudges his own. 'I dreamed you were a door and that you shut,' he tells her again. It seems important. Moss and Hazel begin to cry. They won't stop for a long time. Elvis knows this. He goes outside to play. After a while Moss blows her nose.

'Never mind. I expect things will work out. You might even find what your story is. Find a plot.'

'So you do understand.'

'I always have.'

Outside in the garden Elvis may be seen hitting a tennis ball up against a wall with Moss's old tennis racquet he'd brought back from his Granny's.

'You'll be all right?'

'I expect so. Yes. I will.'

'I love you. Since we were tiny. Since my mother told me you were a pervert. But it hardly ever works out does it. Love?'

'Yes it does. You're just too impatient to wait and see. You have to stay around. Find out.'

'I know.' Hazel kisses Moss quickly and goes upstairs to pack.

'Don't forget to take your Eskimo suit,' calls Moss, thinking of the space her new dress-for-success clothes will need. And all those library books. She supposes it's too much to ask Hazel to take them back, but she says she will, on her way to Heathrow.

Moss and Elvis wave away the taxi in which are two suitcases, the Eskimo suit, many carrier bags of library books and Hazel.

'Don't forget to wear your hat,' cries Moss, thinking of beaches, melanomas and ultimate loss.

'It's just us now, then, is it?' Elvis wants to know. He still clutches the wedding photograph.

'Just us,' says Moss.

And that will do, she thinks, as she goes indoors to fetch her handbag because now, at last, she can go shopping.